PERSEPHONE'S CHOICE

Yihan Sim

Marshall Cavendish
Editions

With the Support of

NATIONAL ARTS COUNCIL
SINGAPORE

© 2021 Marshall Cavendish International (Asia) Private Limited
Text © Sim Yihan

Published by Marshall Cavendish Editions
An imprint of Marshall Cavendish International

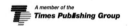

A member of the
Times Publishing Group

Other Marshall Cavendish Offices:
Marshall Cavendish Corporation, 800 Westchester Ave, Suite N-641, Rye Brook, NY 10573, USA • Marshall Cavendish International (Thailand) Co Ltd, 253 Asoke, 16th Floor, Sukhumvit 21 Road, Klongtoey Nua, Wattana, Bangkok 10110, Thailand • Marshall Cavendish (Malaysia) Sdn Bhd, Times Subang, Lot 46, Subang Hi-Tech Industrial Park, Batu Tiga, 40000 Shah Alam, Selangor Darul Ehsan, Malaysia

Marshall Cavendish is a registered trademark of Times Publishing Limited

National Library Board, Singapore Cataloguing in Publication Data

Name(s): Sim, Yihan.
Title: Persephone's choice / Yihan Sim.
Description: Singapore : Marshall Cavendish Editions, 2021.
Identifier(s): OCN 1242908650 | ISBN 978-981-4974-04-2
Subject(s): LCSH: Hades (Greek deity)—Fiction. | Mythology, Greek—Fiction. | Florists—Fiction.
Classification: DDC S823—dc23

Printed in Singapore

CONTENTS

PROLOGUE

Hades landed on Earth with a giant migraine.

Groaning, he clutched his head in agony. His skull felt as though it was cracking open from the inside. He could not open his eyes. The sun seared his retinas through his eyelids, setting off a phantasmagorical display of fireworks in his visual field. His knees protested as he shifted his weight off them and eased himself into a sitting position instead.

"Eh! You okay? You okay?" a plethora of voices chorused in the vicinity.

He had attracted a small audience.

The flashes of light and shimmering stars slowly cleared from his vision as he forced himself to breathe more evenly. The sun no longer seemed too bright. He dropped his hands from his head, forearms falling easily to rest on his knees, and opened his eyes.

A small huddle of concerned passers-by peered anxiously into his face. A few hands hovered uncertainly over his body, careful not to actually touch him, as though he were on the verge of shattering.

"What happened? Did you fall down?"

"You feeling okay?"

"Does it hurt anywhere?"

"Should I call an ambulance?"

On that last query, Hades started.

"No, there's no need," he waved his hand about hastily. "I tripped and fell. It hurt. But I'm feeling better now. Just … leave me to sit here and rest for a bit."

The onlookers glanced at each other doubtfully. *Here* was a stretch of slightly dirty pavement right beside the noisy rear end of a neighbourhood hawker centre. A row of rubbish bins lined a stained wall. A rotund turquoise gas tank punctuated the corner like a jolly garden gnome. The adjoining hawker centre itself was rife with bustle and activity, but where Hades sat, it was relatively quiet. A nondescript back alley. Nobody saw him land.

"Are you sure? It's really no trouble. You should go to the hospital and get checked out. You might have a fracture or something."

Hades smiled at the kindly humans. "Thank you. There's really no need. I just need to rest for a bit." The plethora of solicitous gazes and well-intentioned beseeches were making his head throb.

A clear female voice cut through the knot of bystanders like a bell.

"Come, there's no need to fuss. Sir, you can come in to my shop to rest. It's just over there," the owner of the voice, a petite young lady with short neat hair, pointed emphatically at a little flower shop nestled in the corner of the shopping mall directly opposite the hawker centre.

Hades looked up at the voice. It was gentle, but firm. A cool breeze cutting through the feathery leaves of a casuarina. An overwhelming wave of *déjà vu* nearly felled him. He felt as though he had met her before. Somewhere. In a different lifetime.

In many lifetimes.

He flicked his head as though to clear the haze of confusion that had settled on him.

Why am I here, now, in the mortal world?
I am looking for something.
What am I looking for?

His head was aching again. He could feel an insistent throb radiating from the left side of his skull. His vision threatened to give way again to a constellation of stars.

The young lady had reached his side. Her body was small and feline. There was a practiced grace in her upright posture, suggesting a subtle maturity. She knelt on her knees so she could look into his lowered face, unheeding of the dirty ground beneath her long skirt.

Her eyes were luminous and bright, a playful glint hiding in their corners. She had placed a hand beneath his elbow.

"Come, it's nice and cosy at my flower shop. We have a small space for tea and snacks. You can rest there until you feel well enough again."

As Hades returned her gaze, a sense of compulsion welled up deep within him. There was something he was meant to do in the mortal world. And yet, his brain appeared to be pulsing distractedly and seemingly robbed of all memory prior to that moment. The young lady's mild insistent touch was compelling. He was drawn to her, like a moth to a candle.

I am to follow you.

"Huh?" Hades exhaled at that strange thought. Where had that come from?

"Huh?" the young lady echoed. "What's wrong?"

Hades groaned inwardly. So, he had indeed said that out loud.

"Nothing," he said, trying to smile in a non-threatening manner. "Thank you so much. I appreciate it."

The crowd promptly disappeared once they saw that the injured man was safely ensconced in someone's care. As the space emptied out once more, Hades noticed that the young lady was accompanied by a tall, bespectacled, unassuming-looking man. He was following her around like a puppy.

The two of them supported an elbow each and helped Hades to his feet. The trio walked slowly to the flower shop. Myriad scents enveloped them as they neared. It was comforting and peaceful, like all of spring compressed into a tiny space.

Hades looked up at the sign – SOPHIE'S WORLD.

"My name is Sophie," the young lady smiled up at him. She was a whole head shorter than him. Her little button nose was slightly upturned.

Hades was once again hit with a devastating sense of *déjà vu*. He could not for the life of him place his finger on where he had met her. But that day, she was no more than a stranger.

"I'm Hades," he replied.

ONE HOUR EARLIER

1 SOPHIE'S WORLD

The wind chime sounded its bamboo chortle. The door to Sophie's flower shop creaked open, revealing an apologetic-looking man. He adjusted his spectacles as he entered, bowing his head. He was tall, but not so tall that bowing was necessary to avoid hitting the door frame. Still, he bowed each time he entered, reverently, as one would on visiting a shrine.

Sophie smiled. "Hello, Mr Chang!"

Mr Chang lifted a hand in greeting. He was a regular and walked straight up to his usual stool at the counter where Sophie stood. She reached out to receive the black laptop bag he carried every day and stowed it under the counter in a single fluid motion.

"Would you like to try my new recipe today? It's cherry blossom tea. I finally found a place that sells pickled cherry blossoms," Sophie pattered cheerfully, picking up a brown side-handled teapot and its matching teacups. The striated clay teapot was simple and understated but for a seemingly accidental bright splash of persimmon paint at the end of its spout.

"Thanks, Sophie," he smiled reticently. Hopping onto the tall stool, he nodded politely to the other customer seated by herself at the far end of the counter, right next to the window.

The woman was in her mid-thirties. She was nursing a tea while reading a thick paperback novel, occasionally glancing up at the swaying tree branches outside the window. She smiled back at him faintly.

Sophie's flower shop was a peculiar little place. A cosy nook tucked some way from the bustling main street, it was refreshingly dim and quiet. Unlike typical flower shops, it did not carry the cloying smell from an abundance of fresh blooms. Ironically, it smelled mostly of dried flowers. Twigs. Herbs. Grasses.

The dead given new life.

The walls were decorated with handmade dried floral wreaths and wildflower bouquets hung upside down. They appeared almost haphazardly arranged, accentuated with rough muslin, twine and burlap ribbons. There was lavender, pine, daisies, wheat, white gypsophila, soft brown thistle, the palest pink bunny tail grass … One could sit at the pinewood counter cradling a steaming cup of tea with a small bowl of rice crackers and not notice a hundred years pass by outside the small modest windows.

The fresh flowers were carefully stowed in an opaque refrigerator behind Sophie's cashier till, with more in a hidden backroom prohibited to customers. It was almost as if their dewy exuberance were a vulgar affront to the soft whispered colours that made up the rest of the flower shop.

"Here," Sophie trilled happily, as she presented a hot cup of cherry blossom tea.

Mr Chang exclaimed. A single, elegant cherry blossom had unfurled its petals in his teacup. It floated serenely just beneath the surface, its petals' light rosy core radiating outward to an ethereal, translucent white. The cup was carefully placed on a small square rattan coaster. Its overall effect against the aged wood of the countertop was captivating.

"It's just too beautiful to drink," Mr Chang laughed.

"Oh, come on! That's what you said the last time about the osmanthus and wolfberry tea in the glass tea set! If I do recall correctly, you had two whole pots of it," Sophie tried to keep the mischief from her voice.

Mr Chang made his usual laugh-cough noise and picked up his cup.

"So," Sophie leaned her elbows conspiratorially on the counter. "How was Miss Pink Lilies?"

She often referred to Mr Chang's dates by the bouquets that he bought for them from her shop.

The ambiguous laugh-cough again. He turned his head away slightly, averting his gaze.

"Well, you know ... a guy like me ... it's always a stretch."

He had started trying out dating apps three months ago and had been on quite a few dates since. In fact, that was how he came to know Sophie. An old-fashioned sort of man, he had looked to buy some roses to bring along on his first date and chanced upon Sophie's flower shop. *Red roses are passé,* Sophie had informed him in a serious tone, before proceeding to interrogate him for more than an hour about the lady he was going to meet. It was only after she was satisfied that she had a rough understanding of the woman's appearance, personality and interests did she finally start making the bouquet. She was done within fifteen minutes. *A bespoke bunch, specially made for your special lady.* Sophie had then winked and lightly pushed him out the door.

Mr Chang soon came to know that this was her modus operandi for all customers. She refused to sell bouquets before she had thoroughly assessed the facts of each case: the intended recipient, the occasion, the relationship between the customer and the recipient, just as much information as was humanly possible. *I want to make a bouquet that will light up her eyes ... and soothe her soul*, she says.

Sophie's voice broke his reverie. "What do you mean, a guy like you?" She sounded genuinely confused.

The laugh-cough again. Mr Chang self-consciously combed his thinning hair with his fingers and nudged his spectacles with his knuckles.

"Objectively speaking, I'm not much of a catch." Mr Chang peered into his teacup. The cherry blossom petals were breaking apart. "I'm not handsome, I don't have an impressive job ... I don't have a car."

Suddenly on a roll, he continued. "I'm already forty. I don't foresee myself achieving anything spectacular in my career. Sure, I have some savings and I know how to make use of sensible financial tools to stretch them. But this would be to take care of my parents as their needs grow. I really ... don't have much to offer."

It was the longest Mr Chang had spoken in a while. He felt almost out of breath. He took a sip of the cherry blossom tea. It was warm and fragrant, edged with a tiny bit of saltiness that tasted like a secret.

Sophie was listening intently.

"Mr Chang, you're describing yourself like an item for sale in a shopping catalogue. Listing all your technical specifications like that ..." she trailed off.

"Now that you mention it, online dating is not so different from online shopping, isn't it? Putting yourself up as available, detailing your specifications, consenting to being listed in a catalogue to be browsed and assessed by potential partners … There is no difference. I am a product for others' consideration. The date is the interview … no, the test drive!" Mr Chang chuckled, a genuine laugh this time.

"Is that really how it is out there?" Sophie mused softly.

"Of course. Well. I can't complain, I guess. I'm doing the same to the ladies. I am, too, browsing the shopping catalogue, picking out ones I like, ignoring ones I think I would not like. I'll be honest – it was exhilarating at first. All these beautiful women that I would never otherwise have been be able to meet in real life! Certainly not at my workplace in the shipping and logistics industry."

Mr Chang stopped and looked away again. "There has to be someone who is right for me, who would pick me, out of all the other male 'products' on offer, don't you think?"

His tone was rueful. He raised his teacup again.

"So, I take it that Miss Pink Lilies gave it a pass?" Sophie matched his tone, gently.

"She said that she wanted to take things slow. She did not want to rush into a relationship. I have the feeling that she is still … shopping around. Browsing thoroughly before settling on the best possible deal. At the end of the date, I wished her the best of luck and hoped that she would find the perfect man. I don't intend to contact her anymore."

"Which is why you are here today!" Sophie said brightly. "You need a bouquet for tonight's new date."

"Ah … yes," Mr Chang laugh-coughed. "Nothing too

fancy today, please. I've not chatted with this one online for long. Hey, Sophie, how many bouquets have you made for me over the past few months? I think I've lost count."

Sophie rested her chin on her palm. She was thinking, but not about the bouquet sales figures.

Eventually, she broke her long silence.

"Mr Chang," she said, very seriously.

"What is it?" he was slightly alarmed.

"Have you heard of something called the choice overload effect?"

Mr Chang shook his head.

"Well, I once came across a study by a few psychologists. They had conducted an experiment demonstrating that, contrary to our common belief, having more choices does not make us happier. It's in fact the opposite. Having more options leads to increased unhappiness and dissatisfaction."

"Is that so? And how do they show that?"

Sophie frowned a little, trying to remember the details. "There are a few types of experiments. The only one that I can remember is that … when there were two groups of participants, one group presented with six flavours of jam to choose from, and the other group with twenty-four flavours, the group with the twenty-four choices found it extremely difficult and frustrating to make a decision compared to the group with only six choices. And … it's not just about making a choice; afterward, compared to the other group, members of the group with twenty-four options were more dissatisfied with the jam they did eventually choose. Also, this group was more likely to have members who gave up and did not choose any jam at all."

"So the group with only six options found it easier to choose a jam, and were generally happy and satisfied with their choice afterward?" Mr Chang ventured.

"Yes, I suppose so," continued Sophie. "This study stuck in my mind because I guess … I do feel the same way. Feelings of regret are more likely to arise when I pick something out of many comparable options. I would question myself if I had made the correct choice, and imagine what would have happened if I had picked something else. I would also worry that I had made a wrong choice, that another option might have suited my needs better."

"You feel so strongly about jam?"

Sophie burst into laughter. "It's not jam I'm talking about! But it's not a potential life mate either. I don't know. I can't put my finger on it right now. But I've definitely experienced it."

"A school to attend. An industry to lay down roots in for your career. An apartment." Mr Chang volunteered. He was beginning to understand her train of thought. A happy life required some constraints.

"Many of the things I love most in my life were not chosen, or cannot be chosen. And if I were to imagine having had the chance to choose them, out of a long list of comparable counterparts no less, then perhaps I would not love them nearly as much." Sophie thought a little longer. "All of the material items I cherish the most, I did not buy them myself. They are things given to me by other people."

Mr Chang lapsed into silence. He was also mentally riffling through the blessings and treasures in his life.

"Mr Chang," Sophie said again in her suddenly serious voice. "Do you believe in fate?"

"No, wait," she interrupted herself. "Fate, not as in the idea that the future is predetermined and that all we are doing is walking down a road that has already been laid out. I mean something more like serendipity … *yuanfen*."

"How is *yuanfen* different from fate? I thought *yuanfen* was just the Chinese definition of fate," Mr Chang scratched his neck.

"The more commonly used Chinese translation for fate would probably be *mingyun*. It encompasses a larger picture of the world and refers to the general flow of events in life. I'd probably have to consult a dictionary, but I'm quite sure that *yuanfen* refers to something a little more specific. Something more delicate and beautiful. It's … the magic of improbability."

Sophie grew more and more animated as she talked about *yuanfen*.

"Just imagine the sheer millions – I don't know – trillions, bajillions, gazillions of possible events that *could* happen in the course of a single life. You could have turned right instead of left on the day you were searching for a florist in the neighbourhood. And we would have never met. You could have met a girlfriend through work or some other place, and have never needed to try dating apps. And we would have never met. Hmm, your parents could have never met. Your father could have turned right instead of left on the day he met your mother. And you would never have been born. Something like that, you know what I mean?"

"So you're saying that the probability of our meeting, or the fact that I had been born at all, is infinitesimally tiny. And the fact that it happened at all is … *yuanfen*?"

"Yes," Sophie was satisfied. "That is exactly what I mean. It is the magic that *this* happened instead of *that*."

"But I don't really see how this would help me," Mr Chang scratched his neck absently again. "Does *yuanfen* exist in the sense that ... there is someone I am meant to get together with? Is it a matter of finding the person I am fated to marry with all certainty? It sounds so old-fashioned. I don't think anyone believes in that anymore."

"Perhaps not," Sophie shrugged. "But, Mr Chang ... have you ever heard of something called a 'useful fiction'?"

Just then, before he could answer, they were made aware of a fairly large commotion outside the shop.

"Help! Someone's hurt!"

Without a second thought, Sophie and Mr Chang dashed out the door.

2 HADES MEETS PERSEPHONE

Sophie could not immediately see the injured person over the messy huddle of onlookers crowding the small alley. There were many solicitous voices chattering all at once.

She heard a male voice.

"Thank you. There's really no need. I just need to rest for a bit," it implored beseechingly.

Then, she saw him. A large man was sitting on the pavement, his head slightly lowered and his forearms propped on his knees. An unexpected image arose in her mind. A wounded warrior resting at the edge of a battlefield, his weight counterbalanced by the upright spear he gripped beside him. Blood was still dripping from the spear's tip, seeping leisurely into the piles of corpses that lay around him, patiently seeking the earth. An image of loneliness and strength.

She blinked. The man in front of her was nondescript. He was dressed unremarkably. His hairstyle was nothing unusual; a shock of tousled black that looked due for a trim. And yet, for such an ordinary man, he seemed to Sophie to carry in every cell of his body the nonchalant confidence of *power*. She could not understand it. It was strange to her that an injured man could give off such an arresting sense of power.

Without any thought, she walked straight up to the man.

"Come, there's no need to fuss," she called out calmly to the crowd. "Sir, you can come in to my shop to rest. It's just over there."

Sophie knelt down beside him to help him up and looked into his face.

For a moment, there seemed to be a jolt of recognition. *Do I know him from somewhere?*

He had the most unusual eyes. Although his eyebrows were fierce dark slashes closing in thickly on his high nose bridge, the eyes themselves were hooded and slightly downturned, giving off the impression of a faraway sadness. They seemed like the eyes of someone she would never understand.

Without knowing why, Sophie felt suddenly shy. She was unsure if she was doing the right thing. Just then, Mr Chang reached the man's other side and took his elbow gently. She nodded at him and they both gingerly helped the man to his feet.

"Come, it's nice and cosy at my flower shop. We have a small space for tea and snacks. You can rest there until you feel well enough again," Sophie found herself reassuring the man brightly.

The man said something in response that she could not catch.

"Huh?" Sophie strained, turning her ear closer in his direction.

The man offered an apologetic smile. "Nothing. Thank you so much. I appreciate it."

When he smiled, the harshness Sophie did not realise she had been perceiving promptly disappeared from his face. He seemed like an ordinary, kind person. Sophie often prided herself on being able to read people easily. But with him, she was not so sure.

"Here we are," she saw him looking at the shop's signboard. "My name's Sophie."

"I'm Hades," he replied.

~*~

"Sorry for leaving you alone in the shop!" Sophie called out to her other regular customer, the one seated at the far corner of the shop, nearest to the window.

The woman looked up from her book and waved her hand about vaguely to indicate that she did not mind.

Sophie and Mr Chang accompanied Hades to the shop counter. He sat on one of the high stools with ease, his legs were so long he barely needed to hop up onto the seat.

"You *are* feeling okay, aren't you?" Sophie peered carefully into his face. "Just let me know at any time if you need me to call an ambulance. It's no trouble at all."

"I'm fine, really. Thank you for inviting me here."

Sophie noticed that his smile reached his eyes. Satisfied, she busied herself preparing a second pot of tea.

Mr Chang returned to his original place, next to Hades. The place felt a lot smaller with the newcomer around. He realised he had not introduced himself.

"I'm Chang," he extended a hand. "You're Hades, right?"

"Yes. A pleasure to meet you. Thank you for your help."

The men settled back in their seats. A small silence emerged, but not uncomfortably. They watched as Sophie drew out her favourite glass tea set, which was entirely transparent and extremely elegant. Her slim fingers were deft and nimble as they handled the fragile-looking accoutrements. From jars she scooped small mounds of peach flower buds and lavender, and nestled them lovingly into the glass teapot with the small wooden ladle. Her left hand discreetly drew back the long flowy shirt sleeve of her working hand, ensuring it would not get in the way. The small gesture drew the men's eyes to her slim pale wrist. Next, in went the hot water, which trickled like a gentle river. The sound was crisp in the shop's cool stillness. Finally, she picked up the lid by its little orb using only two fingers and softly placed it on the pot.

"Here, try this," she said, as she set the teapot down unhurriedly in front of Hades. "Oh, but let it steep for about five minutes first."

She rooted around her cupboards and drew out a large glass mug that looked much sturdier than the tiny round double-walled cups that matched the teapot. She offered it to Hades. He accepted it with gratitude, relieved at not having to manoeuvre delicate little cups.

The flower shop was a haven of calm and peace. Hades felt his pulse slow gradually.

"I'm sorry, please don't let me interrupt what you were doing earlier," he added quickly, as he felt Mr Chang start to fidget slightly beside him.

"Oh gosh. What indeed were we talking about?" Sophie smiled at Mr Chang. "You were telling me about the bouquet you needed for tonight, right?"

"Yes, no problem, it's no hurry," Mr Chang replied gratefully.

"You know what you have to do ..." Sophie raised an eyebrow.

Mr Chang took out his smartphone and called up the app he had been using. He scrolled to the profile page of the lady he was going to meet and handed the phone over to Sophie.

She bowed her head as she accepted the phone lightly, her free hand again moving to her wrist to hold back the sleeve. She read the profile very seriously, brow furrowed in intense concentration. The trio descended into silence as they waited. Hades became aware of the subtle music that played in the background, tender and tinkling, at a volume so low it was almost imperceptible. But it *was* perceived, consciously or not, and was part of the many instruments of refinement that gave the place its otherworldly calm.

Sophie was still gazing at the smartphone screen, even as the automatic screensaver mode kicked in and the woman's profile page disappeared. Her eyes were reflected in the dark mirror of the screen, glazed and faraway. She had retreated into the inner theatre of her mind, envisioning her creation as she planned it mentally.

Hades could not help staring at the long elegant line formed by the nape of her neck flowing into the gentle slope of her shoulders. She sat ramrod straight, but with her head slightly bowed in contemplation. She gazed upon the blank phone screen as though it were a koi pond.

"Okay! I've got it!" Sophie startled Hades as she abruptly snapped her head up and smiled happily at both of them.

She returned the phone to Mr Chang and started working on the bouquet. Opening the big heavy doors of the refrigerator behind her, her hands flitted like a pair of butterflies around the fresh flowers arranged neatly inside. *Two stalks from here, one from there and one from … no, not this one.* She opened the adjacent refrigerator and hurried around, plucking flowers out so fast the men could barely register her motions. She then ducked into the backroom for several minutes and returned with some fillers and greenery to accentuate the focal flowers. There were at least four different types of flowers in total, all of which Hades could not identify. She had kept the colour palette to strictly lilac, blush pink, white and dark green.

Moving even more quickly now, Sophie picked up her cutters and proceeded to snip the ends of each stalk, adjusting the composition of the bunch and differing heights of the flowers as she went along, pausing every so often to view it at arm's length, and then continuing again. She trimmed edges here and there where required, narrowing the whole lot down to the harmonious shape she saw in her mind's eye. The bouquet was turned this way and that, clipped from the left and from the right.

The clicking, rustling and snipping sounds filled the air with the aroma of fresh gerberas. The shop looked like a proper florist's shop for the first time since Hades entered. Shorn petals and leaves littered the floor all around Sophie as she worked but she paid them no heed. She was laser-focused on the bouquet she was sculpting and on nothing else. Mr Chang knew better than to make small talk whilst she was working and kept up a studious silence as he watched. Hades wisely followed suit.

Finally, after what seemed an eternity of cutting and fine-tuning, Sophie had the bunch of flowers in the silhouette she wanted. She carefully wrapped it in silver-grey paper and secured the bouquet with a ribbon that looked like it belonged on a ballerina's pointe shoe.

"I'm done," Sophie beamed and held out the finished product to Mr Chang.

It was beautiful in an understated and modest manner, neither too big nor too conspicuous, just right for a first date.

"This is a really good one today, Sophie," Mr Chang whistled, turning it around. It felt small and natural in his hands. "Thank you so much, as always."

"You're welcome!" Sophie's face was flushed and lit with an inner radiance. "I enjoyed making it. Please have a good evening! Good luck!"

Hades found himself unable to look away. He traced her happy face with his eyes as she bustled at the cashier's till with Mr Chang's payment. She crouched down to retrieve his laptop bag stowed beneath the counter, her motions unheeding and carefree like that of a young girl's. With a cheery wave, she bade goodbye to Mr Chang.

Before she could catch him staring, Hades spoke.

"Why do you run your flower shop this way?"

"Hmm?" Sophie turned to him. Her eyes were still bright with a rare sort of pure happiness. He could not remember when he last saw an expression like that.

"What way?" she continued, as she went off to fetch her broom and dustpan.

"I mean, I'm no expert in florists. But I would have assumed that customers picked from bouquets made in advance, displayed in a refrigerator with a glass door. Or picked designs from pictures in a brochure. Something like that."

Sophie thought for a moment as she swept up the excess material on the floor.

"I've always wanted to do it this way. It's fun imagining the person who is going to receive the flowers and then creating something that will bring him or her ... happiness," Sophie hesitated. "I'm sorry. It sounds silly and naïve. It's just something that I like to do. Most men who come in to buy flowers for someone they love know nothing about flowers. While I, on the other hand, know a lot about flowers. So, it's only natural for me to help them create a bouquet that the recipient would like."

"Isn't it more economical to have them choose from pre-set designs? That way, you can cut down on waste."

"Well," Sophie tried to think of a way to explain it to Hades. "There is no waste, or at least, no more than any typical florist would generate. When I order the flowers, I have an idea of the range of bouquets I would make, depending on the time of the year. And the type of bouquets I make varies slightly from month to month, depending on festivities and special events. But even so, I don't like to stick to any sort of rules even when it comes to typical occasions, like Valentine's Day, or Christmas, or even for specific life events, like weddings, bereavement, baby showers, birthdays, get-well-soon things ... I guess I just make what feels right for the person each bouquet is meant for."

"Don't certain flowers mean certain things?" Hades smiled lightly. "Ninety-nine roses for 'I love you'? Carnations for condolences?"

"No," Sophie shot back emphatically. "I don't want to speak that language. I don't want to consign entire flower species into narrow brackets. Sure, people sometimes use flowers to say things that they want to say. *I love you. I'm sorry. Get well soon. My deepest condolences.* But I can use flowers to do that without having to follow a set of arbitrary rules that dictate which type of flower should be used for which message. The overall mood of the bouquet is far more important."

She stopped herself. "I'm sorry … I think I'm coming across too strongly. Some people have told me I'm too stubborn sometimes."

Hades rubbed his chin. "Nah. I like your style much better." He grinned conspiratorially.

"Thank you," Sophie beamed, the light coming back into her eyes. "I look forward to creating bouquets for you, if you would let me."

They were briefly interrupted by the other lone customer who had been reading her book by the window. She approached the till to make her payment for her tea.

"Thank you so much. I had a wonderful afternoon, as always," the woman said.

"Please come back anytime," Sophie smiled and waved her goodbye.

She checked her watch. It was approaching eight o' clock.

"I'm sorry, Hades, I have to close up soon. I need to be back before the nurse leaves," Sophie said apologetically, reaching for his empty mug and teapot.

"The nurse?" Hades inquired.

"Oh, for my mother at home. She has dementia and requires care during the day when I'm at work," Sophie explained.

She washed the mug and the teapot as she spoke and dried them dotingly with a hand towel before setting them aside. She looked up, confused.

Hades was still sitting in front of her, with a woeful and contrite expression on his face. "I'm sorry, Sophie, I don't have any money to pay for the tea."

"Oh! That's not a problem! You are my guest after all!"

"I've imposed on you so much today. But the thing is …" Hades scratched the back of his head. "There's something else I need to tell you."

"What is it?"

"I can't remember who I am."

Sophie froze in the midst of wiping down the countertop.

"What?" she asked, wondering if she could have misheard what he had said.

Hades looked extremely apologetic as he leaned forward towards her, his hands crossed on his forearms. "Since I had that fall earlier this afternoon, I have been having trouble remembering … who I am."

Sophie blinked. He had simply repeated what he said before, albeit in a longer sentence.

"What do you mean you can't remember who you are? You said your name is Hades. Were you lying? Is that not your name?"

"I remember my name. But that's about it. I don't know why I'm here, what I've come here to do. I know I'm supposed to do something. In fact, I'm *meant* to do it. But when I try to remember what it is, my mind just draws a blank."

"Erm," Sophie paused. She turned the dishcloth over and over in her hands. "Do you know where you live? Who you live with? Who are your family?"

Hades fell silent. "I've been trying not to panic this whole afternoon. But I can't remember any of that. It's as though the facts have dropped out of my head. I thought that resting here for a while would help me recover. That it's only a momentary lapse. But right now, I'm still drawing a blank."

"Erm," Sophie repeated. She squeezed her eyes shut as she thought hard, a fist pressed to her temple.

Amnesia. Amnesia, amnesia, amnesia. Perhaps he hit his head when he fell. Perhaps he has a concussion. He needs to go to the hospital.

"Hospital!" Sophie exclaimed suddenly.

Seeing that she had alarmed Hades with her outburst, she stopped and tried to calm down.

"Don't worry, Hades. You just need to go to the hospital, get checked out by a doctor, get a CT scan, and they'll figure out what's wrong and how to help you," Sophie said as calmly as she could. "I don't drive, so I can't take you there. But I could call you an ambulance. Or a taxi. I don't know if we should be calling an ambulance in such a scenario. Ambulances are only for emergencies, aren't they?"

She was starting to feel afraid.

"I'm sorry, I'm in no a position to help you. Please let me call a taxi for you," Sophie said.

"I can't go to a hospital," Hades responded. "I don't have any form of identification on me. I don't know who my family is."

Sophie checked her watch again. It was only five minutes to eight now. She did not have the time to travel to the hospital with Hades, get him admitted using her identification, and travel back home. Her mother needed her. But she was the only one who could help Hades. He had nowhere to go now and no one else to call for help.

"Are you sure you don't have anything on you? Any phone? Wallet? Name cards?" she ventured, staring at his attire. His long-sleeved black shirt accentuated his broad shoulders and tapered down to a neat waist. Belt, cargo pants …

"Pockets!" Sophie nearly yelled. She ran out from behind the counter and plunged her hand into one of his trouser pockets. Her hand hit a wall of thigh, muscle-bound and hard as concrete. His pocket was right next to his crotch.

Hades looked down at her in amusement. At that moment, Sophie realised with horror how improperly she was acting. She withdrew her hand from his thigh with a small squeak.

"I'm sorry!" she fairly shrieked in embarrassment. "I didn't mean to do anything sleazy. I got ahead of myself. Erm, perhaps you could check your own pockets. I'm so sorry to be rushing like this, but I really do need to get home."

Sophie's face had turned bright red and she quickly looked away. Hades tried his utmost best not to laugh.

"I've checked them myself earlier," he explained. "I'm sorry but it seems that I really have nothing on me at all. Well, I'm definitely not your problem. I'll figure something out. I'll let you close up now. Again, I'm so sorry for delaying you. Please apologise to your mother for me as well."

Sophie was still turned away from him in embarrassment.

"Sophie," Hades impulsively placed his hands on her shoulders and turned her to face him. "Please don't worry about it. I'm sorry to have imposed on you. I promise I will be fine and I'll figure something out. I just want to thank you properly for your help this afternoon."

She finally met his eyes.

"Thank you, Sophie," he said.

Sophie groaned inwardly. She knew she could not bear to leave him all alone, with nowhere to go for the night, not knowing if he would be safely admitted and settled into the hospital, even if she paid for his taxi fare there.

She heaved a huge sigh.

"You, listen to my instructions," she said sternly.

Hades gave her his full attention. "Yes, Ma'am."

Sophie sighed again. "You will come home with me now. You can sleep on our couch tonight. Tomorrow morning, I will accompany you to the hospital and get you admitted and assessed. Sounds good?"

"You would do that for me?" Hades was surprised.

"Yes, I will do all that. I just said it, didn't I? So, do you agree?"

"Yes, Sophie, I agree to your instructions," Hades smiled.

As she hurried around, retrieving her bag and keys, and turning off the lights and air-conditioning, she grumbled loudly: "I'll have you know, I have locks on my bedroom door. And on my mum's. And the police station is just a few blocks away. If you are lying to me or up to no good, I have 999 on speed dial."

"And," she added quickly, "I practiced mixed martial arts for five years. I may be a bit rusty now, but you know, it's like riding a bike."

She glared at him warily.

"Sophie, I promise you, if I should harm a single hair on either of your heads, may the heavens strike me down immediately and have me properly dead this time, instead of clunking around like an empty can," Hades raised a hand solemnly.

"*Choy*! Stop that! Stop making such ill-fortuned vows," Sophie swatted at his shoulder irritably, as they went out the door. She was even more annoyed when her hand stung in pain from striking him.

3 GODDESS OF THE HARVEST

"Sorry I'm late, Hanna!" Sophie chimed as she unlocked the door to her apartment and streamed in hastily.

The nurse gave a little wave as she set the last of the dishes on the rack.

"No problem, Ma'am," she replied. Sophie was seldom late. She figured it was probably something important this time.

Hanna turned and started towards Sophie with a damp cloth in her hand. She stopped dead in her tracks when she noticed the man accompanying Sophie. Sophie had never brought a man home. She could not help but stare curiously.

He was tall, athletic, with broad shoulders. Despite his slim jaw and rather delicate features, there was an air of severity about him. However, his eyes were kind and somewhat sad. Striding behind Sophie, clad in black, he looked like a bodyguard of sorts.

"How was Mummy today?" Sophie took the cloth from Hanna. She sat down on the couch, next to a frail elderly lady who still had an empty food tray propped up on her lap.

"Aunty was calm and slept most of the day," Hanna reported, using the local colloquialism for addressing older women respectfully.

She could not help but glance inquisitively at the taciturn man towering over them.

"Oh, Hanna, this is my friend, Hades. He's just visiting today," Sophie took the hint and made the introduction.

On hearing the name, the old lady, who had been staring vacantly into space just moments before, startled and looked up at him sharply. Her slightly milky eyes widened with an inscrutable animosity.

Catching the sudden movement, Sophie turned to her mother and asked, "Mummy! Do you recognise me today? It's Sophie."

The old lady had quickly recovered her frailty. She turned her eyes to Sophie disconcertedly.

"Sophie?"

"Yes, your daughter, Sophie. I'm your daughter, Mummy."

"Yes, I have a daughter," the old lady's face lit up with joy. "She should be coming home from school soon. She's such a good girl. My little daughter."

Sophie's face fell. Not today then. Taking a deep breath and bidding herself to remain calm, she raised the damp cloth to her mother's lips and gently wiped away the remnants of her dinner.

"Yes, your daughter is a very good girl," she said quietly, as she assiduously brushed a stray grey lock of hair away from her mother's face and tucked it behind her ear. "She is a good girl who loves you very much."

"I love my daughter very much," the old lady murmured vacantly, her fingers shaking constantly as she made small feeble attempts to push her dinner tray away.

Sophie furiously blinked away her budding tears. Not today. Not in front of her guest.

"Let me get that for you," she swiftly removed the dinner tray and settled her mother in a more comfortable position, carefully raising her feet onto a small ottoman and surrounding her with plump cushions.

"I'll see you tomorrow, Sophie. Good night!" Hanna called as she picked up her belongings and headed to the door.

"Bye, Hades," she added as she passed by him.

"Thank you for today, Hanna," Sophie turned to wave.

As Hanna bustled out the door, Sophie noticed Hades staring at her mother intently, his harsh brow furrowed. There was confusion in his eyes. He appeared to be thinking very deeply.

"Hades, have a seat," Sophie gestured at an empty chair. "Sorry, I would introduce you, but I don't think it's a good day for my mother. Some days, she would be able to recognise me. But not today, I think."

Hades sat down and leant forward; his elbows propped on the wooden arm rests of the chair. He was still observing the old lady intently, who now seemed to be avoiding his scrutiny. She was gazing emptily at the window that overlooked the common corridor, absently humming a tuneless melody. Her shaking fingers plucked at the braided fringe of a cushion cover.

Sophie baulked a little at the awkward silence that descended upon them. She turned to her mother again.

"Mummy, I have a guest who will be staying with us tonight. He's run into some trouble and needs our help. He'll be on his way tomorrow morning. Not to worry, okay,

Mummy?" Sophie said softly, holding her mother's hand.

"Sophie will be coming home from school soon. Coming home from school soon ..." the old lady pulled her hands away from Sophie and gesticulated wildly, her shaking fingers fluttering in the air like dying moths.

"Shh, it's okay, it's okay," Sophie soothed her mother, running her hands slowly down her bony back. "Everything's fine. Let's get some early rest tonight, hmm?"

She continued stroking her mother's back gently. Gradually, the old lady calmed down and resumed staring blankly out the window. Sophie then stood up and pushed her mother's wheelchair into position. In a single practiced motion, she slipped her hands under her mother's arms, locked them behind her back, and, ensuring her mother's knees were safely tucked between her own legs, swiftly swung her around from the couch to the wheelchair.

She did it so quickly Hades had had no time to react.

"I'm sorry, I would have offered to help, but you were so quick I barely registered it," he said.

Sophie smiled at him. "Please don't say that. I'm used to this."

He was caught off guard by the warmth in her eyes. In that moment, he saw the quiet strength that coursed through her, steady and unwavering.

"Just give me a moment. I'll put my mother to bed," she said, swirling the wheelchair around and heading towards the bedroom nearest to the common bathroom.

The apartment was small and shaped like a square. From where he sat, Hades could see at a single glance the doors to all the rooms in the apartment. Two small bedrooms stood next to each other on one side, with the bathroom and kitchen at the adjacent side.

His mind returned to the old lady's reaction when she had first raised her eyes to him. There was no mistaking it. She had *recognised* him. She clearly knew who he was.

He had to find out what was going on.

While he mused, Sophie had returned. She placed a glass of water on the coffee table in front of him.

"Are you hungry? I think I'm going to order in some food. It's a bit too late for me to cook now …" she trailed off as she saw the expression on Hades' face. "What is it?"

"Your mother … She knows who I am, doesn't she?" he asked bluntly.

Sophie started. This day was getting weirder and weirder. She rubbed her eyes.

"Why do you say so? My mum has been suffering from dementia for … almost six years now. She hardly remembers who I am. Or even Hanna, whom she sees almost every day. Her memories consist of random snippets from the past. Are you saying that you had met her before, a long time ago? You would have been no older than a little boy. I'm sure she couldn't have made the connection, not in her condition now."

She watched as Hades considered this. His body was coiled with tension as he rested his forehead on a clenched fist.

"Hey," she said, lightly this time. "It's late. You must have not eaten in a while. Let's just have dinner and a good rest tonight. We'll figure it out tomorrow, okay?"

Hades raised his eyes. "Yes, you're right. It sounds like a good plan. I'm sorry for imposing on you."

"You don't have to keep apologising," Sophie paused. "This ... moment exists now, and won't be here again."

She gave a little smile. "It's *yuanfen* that our paths have crossed."

~*~

Hades stared at the sliver of moon that peeked through the angled glass shutters on the window. Sighing, he crossed his ankles which extended uncomfortably beyond the end of the couch. Sophie had been kind enough to lend him a spare blanket, but the night was windless and muggy so he had bunched it up under his neck. He rested his head on interlocked fingers, stretching out as best as he could. On the couch, where the mysterious old lady had eaten her dinner earlier.

Do I know her? Did I imagine the look of recognition on her face?

Hades closed his eyes and tried summoning his memories with all his strength. They danced tantalisingly just out of reach, like dandelion spores catching on the wind.

He had not told Sophie the whole truth earlier at the flower shop. He did remember some things. He knew who he was.

He was Hades, Lord of the Underworld, Ruler of the Dead. He knew his place amongst the Olympian gods, his responsibilities, his real home. It has been a very long time since he last visited the mortal realm. It seemed ... a lifetime ago. Or several lifetimes. As with all immortal beings, he had completely lost track of human time, nor could he remember how he first came to be. All he knew was the unending present, the infinity of *now*.

But from the moment he landed on Earth, there had been a feeling of *déjà vu* nagging away at him. A teasing sense that all of this had happened before. There was a path in the mortal world he had once walked, and was now following yet again. All he knew was that there was something he needed to do in the mortal world before he could return to where he belonged.

Dagger.

Hades saw the moonlight glint off the silver of a blade just in time to spring into action. He dodged the sharp edge of the knife, knocked it away from him immediately, and moved swiftly to twist the arm of his assailant. Before he managed to secure the attacker into a chokehold, he realised just in time who it was.

Abruptly, he let go.

It was the old lady. Sophie's mother. She backed away from Hades slowly, clutching her shoulder.

He narrowed his eyes. She was standing upright on her own two feet, her wheelchair nowhere to be seen. The door to her bedroom was open. She had somehow managed to walk so quietly, crossing the distance from her bedroom to the living room, without Hades hearing a single thing. She had succeeded in sneaking up on him.

An old lady, with dementia! Hades pressed his fist to his forehead.

Except … she probably does not have dementia, after all.

He opened his eyes and looked her over. Without doubt, she looked old and frail. Her skin was wrinkled and papery, nearly translucent, with webs of veins showing through. Her grey hair was pulled back into a simple knot at the nape of her neck. But yet, there she stood, unfalteringly, albeit in a slightly hunched defensive crouch following Hades' counter-attack. Her eyes bored into his, steadily and directly. The sickly blank expression from earlier was gone. Hades knew she was lucid and sharp.

"Stay away from my daughter," she hissed at him through gritted teeth. "I know who you are."

Hades continued staring at her as she bent down easily to pick up the knife that he had knocked from her grip. She turned and walked back to her bedroom, slowly but soundlessly. Clearly, her leg muscles were strong enough to not only bear her weight, but to enable her to creep with stealth and finesse.

"Who are you?" he said to her retreating back.

She did not turn around.

4 THE REUNION

Early next morning, Sophie accompanied Hades to the nearest hospital in a taxi. Explaining his predicament to the hospital staff, she managed to get him admitted using her personal particulars and contact details. She signed a form effectively pledging to be his guardian and to pay for expenses incurred should no other family members turn up. After completing the paperwork, Sophie slipped out her smartphone, turned to Hades and abruptly took a picture of him. She nearly laughed as his seemingly perpetual scowl immediately transformed to surprise. She waved cheerfully as he was led away firmly by a nurse, his questioning eyes still scanning her face.

Sophie headed straight to the police station. She made a report of the incident that transpired the day before and enquired if they had received any missing persons reports that matched Hades' description. She showed them the photograph she had taken of him and consented to provide them with a copy. The officer who attended to her promised to contact her should the police receive any missing person report that remotely matched his description. Satisfied that she had done all she could to help, Sophie promptly went back to work.

It was almost mid-afternoon when she opened her shop

for business. Sophie leaned her elbows on her counter and inhaled deeply. The familiar smells and the tranquillity of her shop calmed her, as always. She felt her frayed nerves begin to unwind as she continued drawing breaths deep into her diaphragm. It was simply a matter of time until someone came looking for Hades. Meanwhile, he was safe in the good care of the hospital. She felt relieved.

Absentmindedly, she unlocked her phone and scrolled to the photograph she had taken of Hades. She thought she had caught his usual gloomy expression, but now, in the quiet of her little shop, she looked closer and saw that he had been looking down into her face with what appeared to be concern. There were those sad eyes again. Inscrutable and yet seemingly meaningful. She sighed and scrolled away from the photograph. She was a little glad to have this keepsake, if she never got to see him again.

Her thumb accidentally slipped on the screen and the folder of pictures zoomed its way to the top, revealing the earliest pictures stored on the phone. Sophie smiled wanly as an old photo caught her eye. It had been a long time since she had looked at it. It was one of her in her secondary school uniform, surrounded on both sides by her favourite girl pals at the time. They stood in front of a traditional Chinese pagoda, dwarfed by the faraway mountains looming in the background, which were shrouded by mist as thick as rain clouds. The girls had their arms wrapped around each other. They were all grinning in the uninhibited manner of prepubescent girls. It was a school trip her class had gone on to China when they were fourteen years old. She remembered being so embarrassed then that it had been her very first time travelling on a plane.

Her classmates were astounded at her admission of it. She had barely managed to mumble something distantly coherent about her mother having a fear of flying before changing the subject to something more light-hearted.

The fact was, her mother disliked going overseas and had never taken her on a holiday as a child. She had even been reluctant to give Sophie permission to go on the school trip. She had tried to talk her teacher out of taking Sophie, explaining that Sophie had a sickly disposition and she was worried that Sophie would be an inconvenience to her teachers and classmates if she fell ill during the trip. Fortunately for Sophie, her form teacher had one of the most zealously optimistic personalities she had ever witnessed in her life. Her teacher had proceeded to spend more than an hour long-windedly discoursing on the pedagogical benefits of the short exchange trip, expounding tirelessly on the importance of cultural immersion for the learning and education of students, all while cheerfully reassuring her mother that Sophie would be firmly ensconced in the good care of the teachers accompanying the class. *Why, in fact, Mr Tan, the math teacher, used to work as a nurse in Tan Tock Seng hospital for three years! Everything will be just fine. We will keep in close contact with you throughout the trip and provide you with daily updates on how Sophie is doing.*

Looking back now, Sophie was immensely grateful to her teacher; she must have somehow sensed that the real reason behind her mother's reluctance was most probably some kind of separation anxiety rather than any real debilitation in Sophie's physical constitution.

And so off Sophie had gone, four and a half hours away from her mother by aeroplane, finally seeing with her own eyes another part of the world beyond Singapore's borders; *in the flesh*, instead of merely in television documentaries and picture books. She was fascinated by what she saw. Interestingly, it was not so much the sights and the picture-perfect scenery that intrigued her, but the *people*. Although they were human beings all the same, in Sophie's naïve eyes, they seemed another species altogether. The subtle different ways in which they interacted with their peers; the little diverse habits in their everyday lives; the unexpected cadences in their speech; the unfamiliar undercurrents of their inside jokes ... Sophie had been enthralled by it all. She remembered wishing she could study their cultural differences, investigate the way their society worked, tease out the characteristics unique to their community, the way a scientist would scrutinise a breath-taking discovery of some new species of organism beneath a microscope. Sophie recalled the deep desire that had welled up in her during that trip. If the people in just *this* new country were so different, what about the rest of the hundred and ninety-four countries in the world? Surely, the people living in each different place had *their* own quirks, *their* own idiosyncrasies, *their* own beauties and *their* own flaws. She wanted so badly to research them all, to meet the people from all corners of the globe who were so different from herself, to look upon the multifaceted face of the human race.

She could still remember exactly how she had felt on that plane trip back to Singapore – tranquil on the outside, strapped in securely by her seatbelt, listening to the soft chimes and coughs and shuffles in the cabin; meanwhile, inside her ribcage, the ambition for adventure was swelling so greedily and so powerfully she felt her heart might burst.

She had decided in her head there and then that if there were some occupation that permitted her to make a living studying human societies, she would work so very hard to make it there so she could do exactly that for the rest of her life.

Just then, the door opened, sounding her favourite wind chime and breaking her reverie. Sophie hastily put her phone away and slipped her navy work apron over her head. A heavyset man entered hesitantly, eyes darting around to take in the surroundings. A new customer. Sophie pegged him as a retiree, possibly in his late sixties, and looking to buy a gift for an occasion he was unfamiliar with.

"Welcome!" Sophie called warmly, beckoning him to the counter with a slight tilt of the head.

The man caught sight of the cashier's till and felt himself drawn towards it, seemingly by some invisible force.

"Hi, er, do you sell any fruit baskets? Those get-well-soon kind of hampers?" the customer asked, eyes still flitting around, as if searching for some kind of clue.

"Sorry, I only do flowers here," Sophie trilled cheerfully. "If you like, I can put together a nice basket of flowers to lift the patient's spirits and brighten up the sickbed. I've read somewhere that being around nature really helps with a speedy recovery from illness."

The man scratched the side of his nose. He seemed a little embarrassed.

"Er, well, I don't know, would it be … weird? For me to be giving flowers to … my older brother? He's been hospitalised and would probably stay there for a week. I'm going to visit him tonight."

"If he's staying that long, I'm sure he'd appreciate it. To

tell you a secret, men like receiving flowers, too. They just don't want to admit it," Sophie smiled conspiratorially.

The new customer smiled back. She could see him begin to visibly relax.

"That sounds good. It's just that … I wouldn't know what kind to pick. Or what he would like. And … do you do delivery? Could you have the flowers delivered to his hospital room before my visit?"

"Don't worry! It's my job to create something your brother would like," Sophie reassured him happily. "I'm sorry, but I currently don't have the capacity to manage deliveries. Besides, I'm sure it would make him so happy to receive the flowers from you personally. It makes a big difference, you know?"

The customer looked away. There was uncertainty in his eyes.

"To be honest with you …" he took a deep breath. "We're not on good terms now. We had a huge fight four years ago and I've not spoken to him since."

He lowered his head with regret.

"We didn't mean to prolong the quarrel. We just somehow … didn't get the chance to reconcile. Days and months passed, and before we knew it, we were estranged."

Sophie reached out and laid a hand on his shoulder. They stayed silent for several moments.

The man found words spilling unbidden. "I don't even know why I was so stubborn at the time. I was too proud to apologise. I just didn't want to accept that I was at fault. Still, I don't think it was anyone's fault per se. But, I guess, I'm the younger brother and I should be the one to lay down my ego and show respect. When … when I heard that he had a heart attack and could have died … I felt like the stupidest man in the world. The thought that I could have missed my chance to ever speak to him again … it really scared me. I want to make things right."

Sophie listened without saying a word. Her silence, however, was not superfluous. Instead, she cocked her head thoughtfully, nodded in understanding and kept her hands casually busy; they pottered around purposefully, washing teacups, sweeping up dregs in the sink.

"I understand," she replied gravely. "Let me help you!"

She had made a pot of chrysanthemum tea and set it on the counter. As an afterthought, she sprinkled in some goji berries for good measure.

"It would take a lot of courage for you to set foot in that hospital room tonight. To say what you want to say. To lift this burden from both your hearts. Let me help you with my flowers. Let beauty and grace be the focus of your relationship from now on."

Sophie clapped and held her clasped palms under her chin for a moment.

"So, tell me, Mr …?"

"Sitoh," the customer smiled. "Call me Andrew."

"Okay, Andrew," Sophie smiled back. "Tell me, where did your brother love to travel to for vacations?"

She drew out two teacups and set them on matching saucers. The aroma of the chrysanthemum tea had started swirling deliciously in the air between them. She poured slowly, enjoying the rich gold tint that caught the light prettily.

Andrew was slightly taken aback. "Where did he like to go for holidays?"

"Yes," Sophie trilled. "Was it Europe? America? South Korea? China? Thailand? Vietnam? What sort of places did he like to go to relax and unwind?"

She slid a cup of the chrysanthemum tea to Andrew as though it was the most natural thing in the world. He accepted it unthinkingly, relishing the warmth of the porcelain cup and the floral-scented steam that undulated from its surface.

"It was … Switzerland. He loved the Alpine mountains. I mean, I've never actually been there with him. But I know he went there several times with his family, during the December school holidays."

Sophie clapped her hands again. "That's perfect! I'll make you an arrangement of all the Alpine flowers I have. As he recuperates, he will be accompanied by the memories of the icy crisp air, snow-capped mountains, idyllic villages and the almost-forgotten laughter of his young children."

"And," she added, looking into Andrew's eyes. "Also the knowledge that his younger brother had scaled a mountain of fear to reach him again."

Andrew was glad that just at that moment Sophie had promptly swirled around to start work on the flower arrangement and failed to see the tears springing to his eyes. He sat quietly at the counter, gratefully nursing the chrysanthemum tea that was propping up his world. He was so deep in his thoughts he barely noticed the time slipping by.

"I'm done!" Sophie called triumphantly.

Andrew was shocked to see the pristine floor now littered haphazardly with twigs of all shapes and sizes, and what looked like pine leaves and even entire tree branches. He raised his eyes to the small floral arrangement that Sophie was holding with both hands and gasped.

It was as if a magical woodland creature had traipsed for hours through a wintry forest, gathering all that was good and beautiful and true. The colour palette was subdued; there were only white, silver, brown, grey and varying shades of green. Its overall effect, though, was magnificent. Andrew could see in his mind's eye his brother strolling through a Swiss forest, hand in hand with his wife, their children gambolling and play-fighting just ahead of them. He thought of the hiking boots and trekking poles he had seen at their house. The snow gear that they packed away carefully before opening the house to their relatives for Chinese New Year festivities. The collage of holiday pictures scrolling leisurely in a digital photo frame displayed proudly in the hallway.

"Just a moment," Sophie added, as she ducked into the backroom again to fetch a small rattan basket.

"I've secured the bottom of the flowers in a solution to ensure they will stay fresh for a couple of days at least. The twigs and leaves will be fine, they're dried," Sophie explained as she nestled her creation into the rectangular rattan basket, making small adjustments as she went along. She toyed with varying placements of the twigs, branches, leaves and fillers that framed the delicate edelweiss flowers.

Finally pleased with the results, she placed the finished product on the counter.

Struck by its tranquil beauty, Andrew could not find the words to express his gratitude.

"I'm … afraid to even hold it. I don't want to ruin it," he said eventually.

"Oh, don't worry. I've secured everything in place with

hidden clips and other tricks," Sophie replied. "I think … I could even turn it upside down and nothing would drop out. Shall we try?"

She seized the basket and made as though she would actually flip it over.

"No!" Andrew cried, his hands flying out to stop her. "No, there's no need. I trust you," he added hastily, in a more sedate voice.

Sophie smiled knowingly and handed it to him.

"Everything's going to be just fine," she winked.

After Andrew left, the remaining hours flew by in a haze of small tasks and tying up of loose ends. Soon, Sophie's closing hour descended swiftly along with the setting sun. She untied her apron and lifted it over her head. Shaking it free from the clinging remnants of the day's work, she hung it up neatly in its usual place. Slowing her breathing, she closed her eyes and listened for a moment to the soft background music mixing evenly with the quiet of the shop. Her phone screen was pitch black against the light wood grain of her workstation. There were no calls or messages. She thought about the photograph she had taken this morning, ensconced in the camera roll of her phone. She did not know what to feel. A vague emptiness gnawed at the pit of her stomach.

"I'm just hungry," she announced aloud to no one in particular.

Sophie retrieved her belongings, turned off the lights and air-conditioning, and locked up her shop, as she had done a thousand times before. Yet, tonight, it felt different. It was inexplicable.

Shaking her head, Sophie headed straight home. Hanna must be looking forward to ending her shift. Her apartment was only a five-minute walk from the flower shop, amongst the cluster of public housing blocks that were now several decades old. She had grown up in this neighbourhood. She had walked this route back and forth from the flower shop for so long it felt as though her feet would know the way even if she was blindfolded. She could not even imagine living in any other place nor in any other way.

She mulled over the question Andrew had asked her earlier whilst he was making payment. *Sophie, where do you love to travel to?*

She had not travelled anywhere since her mother's diagnosis. In fact, her mother had started showing symptoms just around the time she was making plans to study abroad. *University of Cambridge. Princeton University. Or perhaps, University College London? I want the best degree in anthropology ever.*

The plans never materialised.

Dementia is a syndrome characterised by a deterioration in memory, thinking, behaviour and the ability to perform everyday activities. There is no treatment to cure dementia, nor to stop its progressive course.

Shifting her shoulder bag slightly, Sophie quickened her pace. She did not understand the maudlin mood that had so suddenly gripped her and unsettled her peace of mind. Of all people, she did not have the time nor luxury to indulge in navel-gazing.

The warm lights of home beckoned. Sophie made a mental note to oil the hinges of the metal gate as she let herself in. Hanna was still in the midst of feeding her mother dinner.

"Oh, hello, Ma'am! You're early today!" Hanna exclaimed, looking up at Sophie and then at the clock on the wall.

"Yes, I owe you for yesterday. Let me take over. You can go home earlier today," Sophie smiled as she shed her belongings and went to her mother's side.

She took the bowl and spoon from Hanna.

"Have a good rest. Thank you for your hard work today," Sophie tilted her head slightly.

"Thank you, Ma'am! Have a good night. See you tomorrow," Hanna beamed.

Sophie turned to face her mother. She seemed serene, rocking slightly back and forth. There was a beatific expression on her face.

"Hi, Mummy, it's Sophie. I'm home," Sophie said softly, spooning a small mouthful of porridge into her mother's lips.

The old lady swallowed slowly and turned to Sophie.

"Persephone," she said, very quietly. "Sophie, my daughter, Sophie."

"Mummy! Do you recognise me today?" Sophie could not help but squeal a little in excitement. "I'm Sophie, your daughter."

"Sophie, my good daughter," the old lady smiled faintly. Her fluttering fingers tentatively sought Sophie's hands.

Sophie set the bowl and spoon down on the coffee table and took her mother's hands. They were so thin and fragile.

She met her mother's eyes. She thought she saw the light of recognition in them.

"Mummy, it's Sophie," she said over and over again, tears springing unexpectedly to her eyes. "I've missed you so much. Thank you for remembering me today."

The old lady raised her shaking hand to pat Sophie on the head. She brushed away the stray tendrils playing around Sophie's face as best as she could and ran her fingers through her hair.

"How can I forget my daughter? My precious daughter, Sophie," the old lady said soothingly, as though comforting a small child. She stroked Sophie's head gently. "Such a good girl."

Impulsively, Sophie embraced her mother. She smelled as she always did – talcum powder and rose water. Sophie could not stop the tears streaming down her face. She was glad that Hanna had already left.

"What's wrong, Sophie? Did someone bully you in school?" the old lady cooed, rubbing Sophie's back as she cried with abandon into the crook of her mother's neck.

"No, no, I'm fine," Sophie eventually gathered herself and dashed away her tears with her palms. "Let's eat."

I suppose these are the moments I live for now, Sophie thought. The moments when she was her mother's daughter again. The moments when the light of recognition came on. This was her reason for existence.

Perhaps in a different life, Sophie would have gone on to chase her old childhood dreams. But not in this life. As Sophie mused about it, she could not find it in her heart to resent anything that was and happened to be. There was nothing, no one to rail against. It was merely the indifferent hand of fate and chance. Only a fool would allow anger, resentment and ill will to take root and grow.

She spooned porridge into her mother's mouth as the moon looked on impassively through the slatted window.

~*~

Three days later, Sophie received a call from the hospital, requesting her to pick Hades up. She closed the shop early and took a taxi down immediately.

"Hey," Hades was lounging in the waiting area beside the nurses' station in the neurology ward. "Long time no see."

He gave a cheery wave. Sophie sighed and sat down next to him. She looked up into his ever-inscrutable eyes. He was grinning faintly, albeit in a rather strained manner.

"Would you mind coming in with me later?" he gestured towards the doctor's consultation room.

Sophie stared at him. He looked back at her unfalteringly, *familiarly*, as though they had known each other forever.

"Go in with you? To ... hear what the doctor has to say?"

Hades nodded. He had turned away and was looking up at the ceiling ambivalently.

"I don't think they've been able to find anything wrong with me," he commented amiably.

"About your family ... I've not had any news yet. The nurse on the phone told me that no one has come to look for you either," Sophie enunciated carefully, trying her utmost best not to come across as tactless or cruel.

"Hmm. So I've heard."

Hades rested an ankle on his knee and leaned back, putting his head up against his interlocked fingers. The hospital chairs seemed way too small for him. A moment or two passed in silence, not uncomfortably.

All of a sudden, he sat up and looked into Sophie's eyes searchingly.

"But you came for me," he said. "Why?"

His face was inches away from hers. Sophie could feel the heat from his body as they sat side by side, legs almost touching.

"Well, the hospital has to get someone to pay for your bills, don't they?" she said irritably, brushing a lock of hair behind her ear self-consciously.

"Will you let me be in your debt? I'll find a way to recompense you," Hades said, still holding her gaze studiously.

Just then, a nurse called out to them. "Mr Hades? Dr Prachi is ready for you now."

"Let's go," Hades stood up.

Sophie followed him compliantly, slightly bewildered at herself. She stared at his back. It was the size of a small country.

The conversation with the neurologist was brief and unenlightening. Sophie learnt that the hospital had exhausted all possible tests in attempting to find the cause for Hades' amnesia. But the results had unanimously and stubbornly established his robust good health. There appeared to be absolutely no discernible physical cause for his memory loss.

"Perhaps it's a psychosomatic issue," Dr Prachi had ventured. "I can refer you to a psychiatrist. You should also monitor your symptoms for, say, three months and come back to me for a re-evaluation, just to be on the safe side."

Sophie completed the necessary paperwork to check him out of the hospital. They sat down at the holding area once more.

"So, that's that," Sophie busied herself with putting her wallet away and tidying the contents of her bag.

Hades was looking at the ceiling amiably again. He seemed well at ease in the uncomfortable plastic chair. His left knee spread unfairly beyond the boundary of his own chair and trespassed into that of Sophie's. Their elbows were touching on the metal arm rests that conjoined the chairs in neat little rows.

"Erm," Sophie cleared her throat. "So, what should we do now?"

"Indeed, that is a difficult question," Hades acknowledged. "I see that an odd turn of events have led us to this peculiar situation."

Sophie glowered at him. His countenance was impossibly calm and gentle despite their absurd predicament. She had never in her life encountered such a strange thing, nor even heard of anyone experiencing anything remotely like this.

Despite herself, she suddenly burst into laughter. She laughed so hard her stomach ached terribly. Passers-by glared at her suspiciously as she rocked with laughter, clutching her abdomen helplessly. Her laughter poured from her like a river rushing a burst dam. She laughed and laughed and could not stop until, eventually, a bout of hiccups took over. Hades and Sophie sat there side by side for a long time, not speaking, waiting patiently for her hiccups to subside.

"Hades, just what am I going to do with you? It's like I've been bound to you by the invisible red thread of fate," Sophie held out her little finger and laid it against his thumb. She was pearlescent against his tanned skin. She quickly took her hand away.

"You know, I'm sure this is just temporary. You will regain your memories soon. Your family will come looking for you and the police will notify me. I've made a report for you, you know," she looked at him, slightly accusatorily.

He was looking at her again with that expression of concern she did not understand. Sophie cleared her throat unnecessarily.

"I suppose, in the meantime, I could bunk in with my mother and rent my room out to you. What do you think?" Sophie risked a small peek at his unfathomable eyes. "Things will probably work out in a few days."

"You would do that for me?" Hades' expression softened considerably. "It seems that I am falling heavier and heavier into your debt."

"Yes, and you will pay me back when you get better. With interest."

"How about I work to pay off some of my debt to you while waiting for new developments? May I work for you? At the flower shop?" Hades asked very politely.

Sophie considered it for a minute.

"Yes, that is a very good idea. I could get deliveries going again. A great idea!" she nodded sagely to herself. "You could work for room and board. I suppose I could easily throw in meals as well if you are a hard worker. I'm a difficult boss to work with, you know?"

Hades' smile reached his eyes.

"Yes," he said slowly. "Yes, boss, we have a deal."

5 DESTINY IS DEAD

Sophie unlocked her apartment wearily, a slew of shopping bags and Hades in tow. Hanna could not hide the surprise in her eyes.

"Good evening Ma'am … Sir," she inclined her head, her gaze darting to Hades involuntarily. He was grappling with the bulk of the shopping bags. They blossomed around him like flowers.

"Hey, Hanna," Sophie said distractedly. "Sorry, I'm a bit late again tonight. I'll explain it all to you tomorrow. Please don't let me keep you!"

"It's no problem," Hanna quickly proffered. "Aunty has just finished eating dinner." She was fairly bursting with curiosity but a quick glance at Hades' grave expression made her hold her tongue.

"Have a seat, please," Sophie gestured to Hades as she swept the shopping bags into her bedroom. It was the one nearest to the front door.

As Hanna packed up her belongings, Hades sank into the same chair he had sat on the last time he was there. He looked directly at Sophie's mother, who was seated neatly at her usual spot on the couch. This time, the dinner tray had been cleared, and a patchwork quilt was laid neatly across her lap. She stared out the window vacantly, a dazed smile playing about her lips. There was no trace of the vigour from the night she had tried to slit his throat.

Sophie spent some time in her bedroom, packing her own belongings for the temporary sojourn to her mother's room. Hades could hear her dragging a *tilam*, a light foldable mattress, out of storage. He was certain that Sophie's mother had to be dying inside to know what was going on. He affixed his eyes upon her face, not yielding even for a second. He wanted to catch that twitch of a muscle, that dart of an eye, anything that would give her away. But the old lady patiently kept her line of sight away from Hades. She was even humming a little indistinct melody. A perfect mask of imperturbable calm, Hades thought.

On completing her packing to accommodate the new tenant, Sophie finally returned to the living room. The silence was deafening.

"Mummy!" she said brightly. "Mummy, how are you today?"

She sat down next to her mother on the couch and took her hands in her own. They were trembling. Sophie gazed absently at their clasped hands for a while, resting against the happy swathes of haphazard cloth making up the patchwork quilt. Her mother had made that quilt for her when she was a little girl. It had been a long time since she was small enough for that patchwork quilt.

Sophie tried to catch her mother's gaze but it appeared to be one of those futile nights. She continued staring into space, seemingly unaware of Sophie's presence at all.

Sophie continued her forced cheerful monologue, undeterred.

"Mummy, you've met my friend Hades before. He's gotten himself into a spot of trouble. I will be renting my bedroom to him until he sorts things out. So, in the meantime, I will bunk in with you, yeah, Mummy? Just like old times, eh?" Sophie shook their clasped hands slightly, wishing for any kind of response. "I'll be your little girl again, sleeping by your side, with this blankie that you made for me."

She ran her fingers along the quilt, its soft worn texture bringing back a flood of memories. There was a song by the Rolling Stones her mother loved and used to sing to her when she could not sleep as a child.

Childhood living … is easy to do…

The things you wanted, I bought them for you …

She hummed the song just then, rubbing warmth into her mother's stiff fingers. There was still no response. The old lady sat quietly, her face blank. She looked almost beatific.

"Where are you tonight?" Sophie whispered, resisting the urge to turn her mother's face towards her.

Wild horses … couldn't drag me away …

Wild, wild horses …

We'll ride them some day.

Sophie watched as her mother's eyelids slowly drooped shut, as sleep came chasing on the tails of her lullaby. She sighed softly.

"Let's get you to bed," she whispered, clasping her mother in her practiced grip and swung her effortlessly from couch to wheelchair.

Hades found that his knuckles had turned white from

gripping the wooden arm rests of his chair. He forced his fists to relax and brought his fingers to a loose clasp between his knees. An unknown fury had arisen in his chest. He felt a familiar migraine gleefully seizing his skull.

Sophie settled her mother into bed. She closed the door and started back towards the living room. She slowed her footsteps as she observed Hades' side profile. His body was coiled with tension, like a serpent ready to strike. He was leaning forward in his chair, an intense gaze directed at the empty spot on the couch where her mother had sat. She wished she knew what was on his mind.

"Hey," she gently laid a hand on his shoulder. "It's been a long day. Let me show you to your room."

As he looked up at her, she saw a visible softening in his expression. Sophie led the way. She had placed the clothing, towels and assorted paraphernalia they had bought together in neat piles on the freshly-made bed. The writing desk was cleared of all items, except for a small reading lamp.

"I didn't want to spend too much time clearing out the wardrobe completely, so, please just use this section only," she tapped shyly on one side of the cupboard. "I still have things in this other half, so … erm … well … I mean, there isn't anything secretive in there, but … I suppose just refrain from …"

"I understand," Hades cut in. "I'll only open my half of the cupboard."

He was smiling lightly in a bemused manner. The room felt a lot smaller with him standing in it. She bit the corner of her lip and handed him the key to the room.

"Here, you can lock up when you leave for work. I'm afraid I don't have any duplicates for the front door, but I suppose since we would get off work at the same time …" Sophie trailed off. She felt suddenly awkward. The circumstances sounded too intimate for someone she had just met for less than a week.

"Don't worry, Sophie. I'll impose as little as possible. You're doing so much for me. I'm grateful."

Hades had laid his hand on her shoulder. Sophie supposed it was meant to be a reassuring gesture, but instead she found a deep flush shooting up to her face. They were standing very close together in the tiny room.

"Alright then! I'll leave you to get settled. Feel free to knock on our door if you need anything," Sophie quickly turned away. "See you in the morning. Don't be late!"

She then fairly scampered out of the room and almost tripped on the edge of a rug in her haste to put as much distance between them as possible.

I'm a grown woman. Get a grip. She mentally chided herself.

Humming the Rolling Stones song under her breath, she did not realise that she was smiling as she hurried around, putting her things away in her mother's room and covering the *tilam* in a clean bedsheet.

Hades had locked the bedroom door before getting into the narrow single bed. The window overlooked the common corridor, so the shutters were sensibly titled at an angle to ensure both airflow and privacy. Still, it bothered him that Sophie had been sleeping in such close proximity to the dangers of the night. He frowned as he stretched out on the bed, an arm flung carelessly across his stomach. The slant of the shutters obscured the moon, but he knew it was there, grinning wickedly down at him.

Hours ticked by, but still, Hades did not close his eyes. He surveyed the room leisurely, as though committing every detail to memory. It was a surprisingly austere bedroom for a florist. He supposed that Sophie brought everything beautiful she owned to her flower shop, instead of keeping them to herself, so that they could be enjoyed and admired by more people. That was just the sort of thing she would do. He looked hard at the small writing desk and the uncomfortable wooden chair that accompanied it. He imagined Sophie seated there. What would she do in her few hours of leisure? Read a book beneath the meagre light of the small lamp? Write a letter? Would she put on her makeup there in the mornings? There was not even a hairbrush left on the table.

Hades heard the sound of a key being inserted and the door knob turning. He sighed, irritated, even though he had been expecting it. *Here she comes.*

The old lady entered, stony-faced. She raised both her hands to show that she bore no weapons, unlike their prior nocturnal encounter. Instead, she was holding what looked to be a children's book. It was square-shaped and fairly large in size, with colourful imagery adorning its cover. The curling pages were time-worn, yet it was clear that the book had been preserved with great care. Hades gazed at her coolly, not moving from the bed where he lay casually atop the covers, still clad in his street clothes, ankles crossed insouciantly.

The old lady closed the door and sat down on the wooden chair, placing the children's book on the table. Her eyes were keen and sharp, with no trace of the blankness she had put on earlier. She sat there for a very long time without speaking. Hades thought he could almost feel the palpable hatred and fury radiating from her like whorls of heat from a wildfire.

Hades sighed and sat up on the bed. He rested his elbow on a raised knee. At that moment, his head was clear and laser-focused.

There was only one thing he wanted to know. "Why are you lying to Sophie?"

The old lady ignored his question and stroked the cover of the picture book idly.

"This was one of her favourites as a little girl," the old lady finally spoke.

She trained her filmy eyes on Hades. "Did she ever tell you her full name?"

Hades was side-swiped by the unexpected question. He remained silent.

The old lady laughed drily. She tossed the book onto the bed, where it caught the sliver of moonlight. That was when Hades saw the title of the book for the first time.

The Abduction of Persephone.

"As she matured, she came to believe that she had liked this book so much as a child because she shared the same name as the female protagonist. I let her believe that. I never once told her the truth."

"The truth?" Hades' hand twitched slightly as he took the book in hand.

"The truth that this storybook is a prophecy," the old lady said very matter-of-factly. "In fact, no, not a prophecy. A *curse*."

That last word she spat out like a gob of sputum.

"You asked me who I was, didn't you? Well, I believe you will find the answer in that book."

The old lady stood up from the chair and switched on the small reading lamp on the table. She gestured for Hades to take her place.

Still reeling slightly from disbelief, Hades placed the book on the table and scrutinised its cover once more beneath the surprisingly strong yellow light of the lamp.

The Abduction of Persephone.

The title was embossed in some sort of flimsy gold paint that had started flaking away badly. The cover design featured a dark, monstrous figure who had flung a beautiful maiden over his shoulder and was striding purposefully towards a majestic chariot that awaited with its four dark horses. The maiden reached her fingers out towards the reader, pleadingly. A crowd of nymphs clutched each other faintly in the foreground; the brush strokes that had painted them were soft and fading. The maiden, however, was illustrated with immaculate detail. Her skin was flushed and rosy as though illuminated by real sunbeams; her lips plump and luscious as though reddened by real blood; her golden hair tumbled down a neat little waist and curled coquettishly at the ends with a strength and grace that was clearly beyond any mortal achievability.

Hades smiled faintly. He could see why the book would appeal to a little girl.

As he opened the hard-backed cover to reveal the first page, a bolt of pain seared through his head, nearly doubling him over. Sparkles of light danced across his darkened vision. *That damned migraine again.*

He waited for the pain to subside. His vision gradually returned to normal, allowing him to focus on the words that had unfolded before him.

Once upon a time …

He shook his head a little, as if physically trying to shake off the remnant floaters in his line of vision.

~*~

Once upon a time, Zeus, the King of the Olympian Gods, had a brief affair with Demeter, the Goddess of the Harvest.

They bore a beautiful baby girl whom they named Persephone. She was beloved by all for her dove-like kindness.

Demeter loved her daughter very much and wished to protect her from the evils and ugliness of the world. She kept Persephone by her side at all times, dressing her in resplendent gowns and accentuating her beauty with the most dazzling gems in the world. Demeter endeavoured to retain her innocence and purity, even as Persephone began to grow into a woman.

One day, Hades, the Lord of the Underworld, glanced up upon the mortal realm above. He saw the glowing young Persephone playing and laughing with the nymphs in a field of gold.

Now, the Underworld was a dark, isolated and forbidding place. It was Hades' job to judge the souls of all the dead. He had so much to do that he was hardly able to visit his Olympian brothers and sisters up above. As time passed, the other gods grew to fear him, and the mortals barely dared to say his name.

Hades was a righteous and just god, but as he silently carried out his duties over the centuries, he grew cold and lonely. His heart was as hardened as stone, turning numb and incapable of feeling.

And yet, as he observed Persephone dancing in the field that day, he was struck by her beauty and tenderness. He returned again and again to gaze upon her, feeling his ancient heart soften each time.

Finally, he paid a visit to Mount Olympus to ask his brother Zeus for Persephone's hand in marriage. Zeus was pleased with the proposal. Hades was the richest and most reliable amongst all the gods. He gave his consent to the marriage immediately.

However, Hades had watched how Demeter doted on her daughter. He knew that she would never agree to give her daughter's hand in marriage to the God of the Underworld.

One day, when Persephone was alone in the field, a great chasm split open in the ground and out sprang a splendid black chariot, edged with gold, pulled by four strong horses. Hades leaned over and swept Persephone up into the chariot beside him. Before she could even scream, they had plunged deep into the Underworld.

Demeter soon discovered that her daughter was missing and searched frantically for her. She soon found a farmer who had witnessed it all. On hearing the turn of events, Demeter grew livid. She vowed that the ground would never produce a stalk of wheat until Persephone was returned to her.

Down in the Underworld, Persephone was distraught. Hades was kind to her and showered her with gifts and treasures, but she missed her mother and the bright world above.

Hades was saddened, but he was also patient. He placed Persephone's throne right next to his, and unlike other gods, allowed her equal rule alongside him. He treated her not as his property, but as someone who could eventually become a friend. When Persephone suggested that he create another realm for the best mortal souls to go to, Hades made it for her. It was called the Elysian Fields – the Underworld's heaven.

Persephone was extremely conflicted. She missed her mother, but Hades was the only person who had ever treated her like an adult. She felt herself falling in love with him.

One morning, Persephone visited the garden of the Underworld. The kindly gardener offered her a pomegranate. Up until that point, she had resisted eating anything given to her, for she knew that if she ate any food from the Underworld, she would be bound to it for eternity.

But that morning, Persephone felt bold and adventurous. She took the pomegranate and ate six of its seeds.

Abruptly, Hermes, the messenger of the gods, appeared before her. He told her that Demeter had caused the earth to freeze over and that no crops could grow. Mortals were dying in droves and the only thing that would stop Demeter was Persephone's return. Persephone reluctantly allowed Hermes to take her to Mount Olympus, where Zeus and Demeter were arguing heatedly. Demeter berated Zeus for promising their daughter's hand in marriage to Hades without her consent.

On laying eyes on Persephone again, Demeter burst into tears. Persephone tried to comfort her mother, reassuring her that Hades had treated her well. But Demeter insisted that Persephone return home with her, or she would let every mortal on earth die of hunger.

At that moment, the throne room darkened and Hades stepped out of the shadows. He held the partially-eaten pomegranate in his hand.

"Persephone has eaten the fruit of the Underworld," Hades said coolly. "She must return to rule it with me."

While Demeter resumed her tirade, Zeus considered Persephone quietly.

"Daughter, how many seeds of the pomegranate did you eat?" he asked.

"Six."

Zeus rose from his throne and the assembly of gods immediately fell silent.

"Since Persephone has eaten six seeds of the pomegranate, I decree that she shall spend six months of each year in the Underworld with her husband, and six months tending to the mortals' fields with her mother."

Neither Demeter nor Hades were completely happy with the arrangement, but Zeus had made his commandment. Every year, Persephone returned to the fields and restored them with Demeter. When the time came, Hades would come to her and escort her back to her throne in the Underworld. Each time she left, Demeter mourned and let all the plants and vegetation die. Each time Persephone returned, the earth warmed and became fertile once more.

~*~

Hades closed the book. *Did I really do all that?* He mused. It all felt so hazy and unreal, like a dream from a lifetime ago. No, *several* lifetimes ago. He glanced at the glorious bident the illustrated figure clutched in one hand. *Now where did* that *go? Probably in one of the forgotten storerooms. Mental note: get the lieutenants to fish it out for old time's sake.*

Hades had always known he was an ancient Greek god, *but heavens*, reading that book made him feel truly old. He barely remembered what it felt like to be that person in the story at all.

He raised his eyes to the corner of Persephone's bed where the old lady was seated. She had waited as he read.

"I suppose, then, you are Demeter, Goddess of the Harvest?"

It was more a statement than a question. Hades swiped at his eyes wearily with the backs of his hands.

Demeter nodded. She held a look of resignation on her face.

"Hades, Lord of the Underworld," she started matter-of-factly. "Our stories ebb and flow with every epoch of human civilisation. When the mortals start telling our stories again, we are called back into existence, and are condemned to live out our destinies, over and over and over again … until the last mortal voice is silenced. It is only then can we finally die, along with our tales."

Hades was silent for a while. He wondered whether some mortal was out there *right now* telling his story. *Why now? Why would mortals continue telling and retelling these ancient stories from generation to generation, keeping them alive all through the centuries? What need do they have of the Olympian gods? What was it that the mortals really wanted, when they fabled the gods into being?*

"I don't think you truly believe in destiny, do you?" Hades asked suddenly.

Demeter met his eyes with surprise. "What do you mean?"

"If you had known that this day would come, that the God of the Underworld would take your daughter away from you in marriage, why would you put on this ridiculous charade? Why would you hurt your own beloved daughter so?"

Demeter stared ferociously. "This is the only way I can keep her safe by my side. You, of all wretched creatures, would never understand a mother's love for her child."

"Love. If this is what you call love …" Hades trailed off, his thoughts suddenly faraway. "If what you are doing is love, I would want nothing to do with it, nor would I wish it on my worst enemies."

"Persephone belongs to me," Demeter hissed through gritted teeth. "I raised her all on my own. I tended to her needs since she was a baby. I alone fed her and clothed her. I taught her the joys and the sorrows of this world. I was there for her through all her pain and suffering. I did everything I could for her. No, *everything I did was for her*. There is no mother on earth who loves her daughter more than I do. And who are you, or any other man for that matter, to blithely stride along and take her away from me?!? I gave her my everything, and now, she *is* my everything. How dare you, a stranger who had never done a single thing for her in her life, come here now to stake your claim on her? Don't you see how unjust it is? How cruel?!?"

There were now tears streaming wildly down Demeter's face. She made no gesture to wipe them away nor to restrain them.

Hades sighed heavily and stretched out his neck, raising his face to the heavens with eyes closed.

"Demeter," he said steadily. "That story is thousands of years old. If you don't truly believe in destiny, then you can choose to believe that the story will not come to pass. Be honest and genuine to your daughter. She deserves that much."

"You understand nothing," Demeter shook her head. "You are merely a hot-headed impetuous young child, just like Zeus was. Do you really think you have the power to alter fate itself? To change the course of the river?"

"The way I see it, this is simply a childish story, created in the infancy of human civilisation, when they groped blindly for explanations of things in nature, such as the passing of the seasons," Hades opened his palms indifferently. "I see that things are different now. Mortals no longer need such stories. They've outgrown them."

"Can you outgrow a curse? Hmm?" Demeter jeered. "Why do you think I have gone to such great lengths just to keep Sophie by my side for a little longer?"

"Because you are stark raving mad, woman!" Hades could no longer contain himself. "I have no wish to abduct Sophie, nor to bring her back to the Underworld with me. I will prove to you, then, that destiny is dead. Fate does not exist. And you have ruined your daughter's life over a stupid children's book."

Suddenly incensed, he thrust the book back into Demeter's hands and strode towards the door.

"Please, it's getting late," Hades opened the door and stood aside emphatically.

Demeter held the picture book to her chest and left the room without looking back.

6 A CHINESE GHOST LOVE STORY

Sophie was worried about Mr Chang. He had been coming in to her shop for a few evenings in a row now, mulling over a pot of tea for an hour each time before hauling himself home heavily like a man being sent to the guillotine. It was puzzling because, apparently, the date with a Miss Lilac Peonies had gone extremely well. They had settled into easy conversation right away, felt comfortable in each other's presence and had a wonderful old-fashioned first date. In fact, they had gone on several other dates after that.

"Are you going to ask her to be your girlfriend soon?" Sophie leaned her elbows on the counter, a mischievous glint twinkling in her eyes.

Mr Chang seemed startled. His hand shook as he placed his teacup back on the saucer. There were dark purple smudges beneath his eyes and his face was pale and drawn. Now that Sophie looked closer, she saw that he was practically emaciated.

"I … I'm not sure. I mean, I'm so happy that I've finally found someone whom I can get along with so well," Mr Chang hesitated. "Sophie, I *really* like her."

"Well that sounds lovely, doesn't it! What's stopping you then?"

Mr Chang fiddled with the teaspoon nestled at the side of the saucer. "There's something I'm a bit concerned about. But ... I'm so sorry! It's hard for me to tell you. It's a little embarrassing."

Sophie looked her friend over, concerned. She hoped that he was not having any problems with his health. He seemed to have lost a considerable amount of weight.

"It's not that I don't trust you, Sophie. It's just that ... the subject is quite ... delicate," Mr Chang stammered on.

"It's alright," Sophie placed a reassuring hand on his wrist. "You don't have to tell me anything. But just know that I'm here to help in any way I can."

Mr Chang smiled gratefully. It was quick to fade, though, and his head drooped once more over the pot of jasmine and honeysuckle tea on the counter like a wilted rose.

The wind chime at the door sounded. Hades had returned from making a delivery. Sophie's face lit up.

"How did it go?" she asked breathlessly.

"It went well," he replied, grinning despite himself. Her excitement was contagious. "I met him at the school carpark and passed the bouquet to him. Then I couldn't help but sneak up to the classroom to watch his proposal. It was ... well done! His girlfriend cried and everything. Her students were cheering and rushed up to both of them for a group hug. All went according to plan. Mission accomplished, Ma'am."

Sophie leant back, not bothering to contain her delight. "Oh, how lovely. I'm so glad."

She had spent hours on that particular bouquet, weaving in the engagement ring in its box as securely as she could. As it was for a marriage proposal, she had made the bouquet as gargantuan as the laws of physics would permit. It was a veritable firework that could be held in both hands.

Sophie was glad to have Hades around, for she could now accept more requests for deliveries. It meant that she could help create more special moments for even more people. And she trusted Hades to get the job done smoothly, no matter how intricate each particular request was. He had hidden in bushes in the dead of the night for a seaside proposal. He had waited patiently in cramped, airless stairwells of hotels and restaurants. He had walked for kilometres in pouring rain to reach a remote location for a funeral. He had navigated the winding corridors of countless hospitals at all hours. She knew she could always count on him to deliver the small pockets of happiness she created.

Sophie handed him his work apron as he ducked under the counter to enter their working space. There was a latched opening that could be lifted to allow entry, but neither of them bothered with it. Sophie watched as Hades put on the apron languidly, as if he had been doing it his whole life.

"I'll tie it for you," she said. "You make really ugly ribbon knots, you know?"

Hades frowned in mock despair. "You're so mean to me, you know?"

He turned around and allowed Sophie to knot the strings of the apron securely behind his back.

"Nobody's going to notice if it's at the back," he pouted at her, imitating a child.

"Oh, trust me, *everyone* notices," Sophie said darkly. She had recently acquired a new breed of clientele, consisting of giggling school girls who lingered for hours over a shared pot of floral tea just to catch a glimpse of him.

A delicate subject.

She suddenly remembered what Mr Chang had said. Perhaps he was shy to tell her his problems because she was a woman. Perhaps he would share them with a man.

"Hades, I have a task for you," Sophie announced.

Hades and Sophie emerged from the backroom after a brief conference. Hades wore the wary expression of someone who had been coerced into performing a dare. Sophie smiled at him pointedly and gestured urgently towards Mr Chang using her eyes.

"You're a bully," he muttered to her under his breath.

"Be a good boy now or you shall go hungry tonight," she whispered back.

Sophie turned her back on Mr Chang and busied herself tidying the contents of the refrigerator. Dishcloth in hand, Hades proceeded to nonchalantly wipe down the sink.

"Hey, man, you got a minute?" he asked Mr Chang casually.

Lost in thought, Mr Chang raised his head dazedly. "Yes, Hades?"

"Chang, it's a bit embarrassing, but do you mind if I get your advice on something?"

"Huh? Yeah, sure," Mr Chang replied, scratching his neck.

"Er … it's kind of … private," Hades said in a low voice, gesturing vaguely in Sophie's direction with a slight tilt of his head. "Could we move to that table by the window for a little while?"

"Yeah, sure, no problem," Mr Chang picked up his tea and hopped off the bar stool.

As the men moved to the other table, Hades caught Sophie's eye. He glared at her fiercely. She merely smiled back offhandedly and resumed her busywork.

"Sorry man, it's kinda embarrassing for me to ask you such a private question. It's just that … since I've not yet regained my memories, you are the only male friend I have now. I was hoping to see if you've had the same experience."

"Hey, no worries, you can ask me anything," Mr Chang said warmly. It had been a long time since anyone had asked his opinion on anything. He felt indeed rather flattered.

The two men huddled in an inconspicuous corner of the shop. It was not busy at that time of day and there were no other customers.

"It's about … peeing. Have you ever experienced this kinda very slight stinging, burning sensation when you pee?" Hades coughed, covering his mouth with a single fist. "It doesn't seem to be anything serious, I mean, there's no blood or anything … Just this nagging little irritating, stingy sensation."

To his surprise, Mr Chang simply replied: "Ah."

"Well, it's not uncommon. I guess you must be quite young that you are only encountering it for the first time now. It's probably just a passing infection. You can easily get it checked out at the doctor's and a course of antibiotics should settle it," Mr Chang continued, shrugging his shoulders.

"Isn't it embarrassing to see a doctor about something like this? I mean, it's so slight that I'm not sure if I'm just imagining it. Maybe it will just go away on its own?" Hades pressed on.

"Nah, I think it's better that you see a doctor about it. Personally, I've never waited for it to simply go away on its own," Mr Chang urged.

"Hmm, I guess you're right," Hades agreed, slumped despondently in his chair. "I just hate to think that I should be having such problems when I'm still so young, you know?"

Mr Chang nodded in commiseration. "Well, they say it all goes downhill from thirty, don't they?"

"Is that so?" Hades looked even more glum. "Do you get all sorts of health grumbles now and then?"

"Well, I've been fortunate that there's really been nothing serious so far. I'm not the fittest I've been," Mr Chang patted his abdomen wanly. "But thankfully, I've not had any major health issues either."

Hades nodded. He leaned back in his chair, balancing his weight blasély on its two hind legs. He furrowed his brow intentionally, affecting an expression of grave worry.

"Don't worry, it'll be fine. Just go see the doctor and get it off your chest, yeah?" Mr Chang tried to cheer him up.

"Yeah, I guess I'll do that. Hey, thanks man, I appreciate it," Hades said.

He still looked so gloomy that Mr Chang could not help but fill the silence with his own words.

"Hey, since we're exchanging man-to-man advice, can I ask you something as well?" Mr Chang ventured. "There's been something that has been troubling me recently."

"Yeah, of course. I'm sure just telling someone would help you feel better."

Mr Chang paused. Suddenly hesitant, he scratched his neck again and fiddled with the lid of the smooth bronze teapot.

"Have you ever had a woman who …" Mr Chang looked away. "Demanded too much of you?"

Hades mulled over his question for a minute.

"What do you mean, exactly? Demanding too much of your time? Being too clingy? Too starved for attention?" he explored.

"Well," Mr Chang laugh-coughed. "In my case, it's quite a specific problem. She … er … she seems to be quite insatiable … in bed."

Hades' eyebrows shot up. He wrestled internally to keep his calm.

"You mean, she wants too much sex?" he said, *sotto voce*.

Mr Chang gave a very loud cough. His fingers twitched as if to scratch his neck again, but thought better of it and returned to his lap.

"Ah," he said. "Ah, yes, you've summarised it all too well. To be honest, I am very confused myself. Before I met her, I'd never thought that there would be such a thing as … too much sex. For a man. I mean, we complain so much about not having it enough as it were. But this lady I am seeing … she seems … different."

"It's Miss Lilac Peonies, I presume?"

"Ah, yes. That's the one. We've been going out for a while now and I really do like her a lot. She is the only one among all the others I've dated through the app who seems to really understand me. She is genuinely interested in me, as a person, and not just as a potential candidate to be ticked off a list. Everything went swimmingly well, until, er … we started getting intimate," Mr Chang stopped and took an enormous sip of tea.

"Hmm," Hades said.

"Don't get me wrong, it's not that I have any medical issues with sexual performance. In fact, er, I'm quite proud of myself that I'm still able to … you know … keep up with her despite being no spring chicken myself," Mr Chang was starting to look flushed. "It's just … I don't know. Tiring. I'm so tired. I've not had a full night's sleep for at least two weeks now."

"Sounds like quite a gal," Hades responded lightly.

"What do you think? I mean, what do you think is *normal*?"

"The normal … amount of sex a person should have?"

"Yeah, like, how many times does the average couple do it a week?" Mr Chang stopped himself. He was suddenly aware that his questions were becoming inappropriate for a mere acquaintance. How inconsiderate of him. Such questions should be taken to a therapist, not a friend.

"Hmm," Hades said again.

Sophie had whispered to him earlier in the backroom that she was worried about Mr Chang's health, that she feared he had been diagnosed with a serious illness. He certainly looked it. His skin was pallid and sallow. The vitality had disappeared from his eyes. He looked like a patient with late-stage cancer, and not someone who had just been having too much sex.

"Have you discussed it with your partner? You know … the proverbial two to tango and all, yeah? If you're uncomfortable with the frequency of your … couplings, you should let her know. And then come to a sensible compromise together. If she loves you, I'm sure she won't leave you just because you want a little less sex, if that's what you're worrying about."

The familiar laugh-cough again. And then: "I've tried. She's … she's apologetic about it, actually. She promises to tone it down. But as night comes around, she becomes something almost like … a wild animal. I can't describe it. Like someone possessed. She would be overcome with frantic urges and would not stop until she has satisfied herself. Many times over. I do my best to please her, but … it's become difficult for me to have a good night's rest."

Hades frowned. There was something suspicious about it.

"Do you mind if I asked you a few questions? You don't have to answer them if they bother you," he said.

"Sure, go ahead," Mr Chang leaned forward.

"Does it seem as though … she needs sex the way a starving man needs food? Do you sense a kind of unusual, otherworldly hunger that is rare in mortal women? As though she is, in some way, *sustaining* herself, her very life force, if you will, through having sex with you."

Mr Chang gasped. He had not told Hades the full truth but what he had just said hit the nail on the head.

"Yes," he nodded vigorously. "I mean, normal people feel sleepy and relaxed after making love, right? It's the complete opposite for her. She seems to gain energy from sex, and only from sex. If she goes a day without it, she becomes pale and weak. I didn't make the connection then, but now that you've mentioned it, it really does seem as though she needs sex to stay alive as much as the average person needs air and food and water. Perhaps it's some kind of addiction? A psychological disorder?"

At that point, Hades' face had grown grim. He knew at the back of his mind exactly what was going on.

"Perhaps you're right. Perhaps it would be good for her to consult a therapist. If you're up to it, you could suggest it to her tactfully and offer to be there for her throughout the consultation. I'm sure she would appreciate it."

Mr Chang visibly relaxed. "Yes, that sounds like a good idea."

Hades glanced at the clock on the wall. "I should be getting ready for my next delivery. Let's talk another time."

"Thanks, Hades. I should get going myself."

Mr Chang made his way to the cashier's till, where Sophie accepted his payment with a cheerful farewell. As soon as the door closed behind Mr Chang, she accosted Hades without a minute's delay.

"Well? Did you find out what happened?" she exclaimed.

Hades hid a guffaw. Her eyes were so bright and curious, like a little puppy fascinated by a new toy. A lock of hair was sticking waywardly out at her right ear, making the resemblance even closer.

"There's something Chang needs my help with tonight. He said that I could get his home address from you. Do you have it?"

"Yes, I do," Sophie said impatiently. "But what *is* it? What are you going to do? Can I come with you?"

"Sorry," Hades said solemnly. "I promised him that I would not tell you a thing until it's all over. You just have to trust me, alright? I will save your friend."

"What? Save?" she squeaked. "Is he in some sort of mortal danger? You're not going to *fight* anybody, are you? If something criminal is going on, we have to get the help of the police."

"Hmm," Hades said. "I suppose it is something criminal of sorts, but *I'm* the judge of that. Not the police, not the courts, not human law."

"What?" Sophie was bewildered. "What're you talking about? You're not playing a prank on me, are you? I was just kidding earlier about threatening your dinner. Don't you dare take revenge on me for *that*."

"Sophie, trust me. I will tell you everything when it's over. Just ... take it as I'm off doing another delivery for you, okay? Haven't I proven my capabilities?"

She felt his steady gaze on her, warm and full of strength. There was no delivery order she did not trust him with. She could always count on Hades to get the job done. There was something about him that lured her into a sense of security. *Perhaps a dangerous sense of security.*

"Alright," she said, grumpily handing him a broom and striding off into the backroom emphatically.

~*~

Right, time to catch an errant soul. Hades thought as he let himself out of the apartment close to midnight. He groaned a little internally. In his absence, he had entrusted the care of the souls of the dead to his lieutenants and Cerberus, his trusty hound. Cerberus was a good boy, but as with all dogs, was extremely susceptible to bribes in the form of tasty treats and other delicacies.

Hades could not help but feel slightly disgruntled at having to do the dirty legwork himself. He was Lord of the Underworld, for heaven's sake! What a disgrace. It had been centuries since he last had to personally intervene in the retrieval of an escaped soul. Perhaps he had been away for too long. It seemed his subordinates were slacking off.

Hades grumbled to himself in his head all the way to Mr Chang's house, failing to notice the little lithe figure that had slipped out behind him and tailed him quietly from shadow to shadow the whole way there.

Sophie tiptoed as softly as she could as she followed the tall, broad silhouette she had grown familiar with. Sweating a little in the humid night, she darted around corners, slunk along walls, and took cover behind lampposts when needed, all while carefully keeping a safe, inconspicuous distance between the two of them. She had never secretly followed anyone before. It was more onerous than she expected. Her feet ached from keeping her weight off her heels. The worry of leaving her mother alone in the apartment nagged away at her. But the last Sophie had checked, her mother had been fast asleep in her bedroom.

Finally, they reached Mr Chang's residence. It was not too far away from her flower shop, about a leisurely fifteen-minute stroll for a lanky man. Sophie's calves were beginning to cramp.

A fairly well-to-do man, Mr Chang lived in one of the terraced houses with its entrance facing away from the main street. It was another few minutes' trek to get to it amongst a cluster of similar houses, all lined up neatly in a row. As Hades walked on the empty road, Sophie crept along the shadowed pavements closer to the houses, shielding herself using parked cars and tall rubbish bins.

"Just what are you up to?" Sophie muttered under her

breath, as she struggled to keep Hades in sight.

He was clad in another of his boring unmarked long-sleeved black T-shirts, with tan cargo pants and a simple black military style belt. As far as she could tell, he was not carrying anything with him. Sophie squinted for a bulge in the pockets, indicating some sort of weapon. But his profile was defiantly lean and streamlined, with no sign of any unusual accoutrements.

Before long, Hades arrived at Mr Chang's house. He pushed on the metal gate gently. It was unlocked. Shrugging, he let himself into the small garden and walked right up to the front door.

He knocked.

~*~

Mr Chang did a double-take.

He thought he actually heard her *hiss*. Like a cat annoyed at some new disturbance.

He was lying flat on his back, his partner straddling him and pinning his wrists to the bed rather aggressively. Before the weird hiss, he had been trying to focus on enjoying himself, even as the woman that Sophie called Miss Lilac Peonies rode him feverishly as if her life depended on it. There was a maddened, exulted glint in her eyes as she moaned and writhed on top of him. From time to time, she tossed her long brown hair aside to kiss him, so deeply and thoroughly as though she meant to devour him alive.

And then, there was that noise. She had flicked her head towards the windows irritably, so quickly that the motion almost seemed to Mr Chang somewhat … inhuman. And then she had actually *hissed* at the interruption. Mr Chang blinked very hard. Her teeth appeared tiny and sharp, glistening peculiarly in her small rosebud mouth. He was having trouble concentrating. He felt himself grow soft inside her.

"Sorry," he mumbled, placing his hands on her hips and hoisting her off him to lie beside him on the bed.

For a brief moment, he could not see her face through the thick veil of her beautiful hair. She was still breathing hard, her hands clenched. *Knock, knock, knock.* There was someone at his door. *At this hour?*

At that moment, Miss Lilac Peonies suddenly twitched beside him. With a speed that utterly bewildered him, she pushed Mr Chang down into the pillows again with a most uncanny strength for her slight build. He could feel her thighs clenching around his hips as she pushed down hard on his chest and brought her lips to his once more, forcefully this time.

"I want you so much … Please …" she whispered into his mouth.

Knock, knock, knock.

Knock, knock, knock.

The person at the door was persistent.

Miss Lilac Peonies screamed in frustration. To Mr Chang's utmost horror, she pitched herself off him and *scuttled* out of the bedroom on her hands and legs like a tarantula.

"Am I dreaming, am I dreaming, am I dreaming?!?" Mr Chang pinched his face desperately. "Wake up now, wake up now!"

Dazed, he looked around his bedroom. Everything appeared all too real.

"Wake up! Wake up!" he willed himself, clenching his entire face and squeezing the muscles around his eyes with all his might.

It was not to be. He could hear screeching sounds coming from the direction of his front door, where a commotion appeared to have started up. Trembling, he quickly dressed and mustered courage from every cell in his body.

Someone is here to help. He thought dimly, desperately, as he made his way through the darkness of his house. He was so scared he could hear his pulse pounding in his head. His bladder promptly announced its existence and threatened to empty its contents right there and then.

What on God's good earth is happening?!?

Mr Chang tried to even out his ragged breathing and willed himself not to urinate. If this was merely a dream, he reasoned, he would wake up to a huge inconvenience.

"I'll, I'll go to the front door, to the front door," he encouraged himself beneath his breath, jogging slightly on the spot. "I will not be a coward, not even in a nightmare."

And so Mr Chang finally journeyed to his front door. Partly because he was so frightened to look at the unworldly creature immediately head-on, the first person he saw was a familiar face, faraway and small beyond his open door, at some distance outside his house. It was pale and contorted in shock, but recognisable all the same. It was Sophie!

And then his brain reluctantly focused on the more dangerous matter at hand. His beloved, beautiful Miss Lilac Peonies was lying on the floor of the hall, body contorted grotesquely and squirming in agony. If she had looked only slightly manic before, she barely resembled anything remotely human at that moment. To top it off, she was keening in a tortured manner, as though great pain wrecked her whole body.

There was a man at the open door. Mr Chang squinted. His face was shadowed.

In a calm, almost bored voice, the man addressed the crumpled form writhing hideously on the floor.

"As your lord and master, I summon you. Soul of the dead, you do not belong here."

~*~

Sophie could barely contain her scream as she contemplated the creature that lay in Mr Chang's hallway. It was woman-shaped, barely. All she could see were flashes of pale arm and teeth and hair as it thrashed about on the ground at Hades' feet. Sophie pressed her clenched knuckles to her lips, willing herself to be silent. All rational thought had fled her brain as her eyes darted furiously from the ashen Mr Chang to Hades, who had his back to her.

Then, she saw the creature reach out one stiff hand, hovering but swift, just about to wrap itself around Hades' ankle.

"Look out!" Sophie yelled, launching herself in his general direction.

As if in slow motion, she watched as Hades turned his head towards her with a look of utter surprise. To *her* own surprise, she saw that Hades had one hand clamped tightly around the woman-creature's arm. As she collided into him, he reached out his other hand and grabbed her around her waist, pulling her into him.

And all was dark.

~*~

It was so dark all around her. Sophie struggled to make sense of what had happened. But her brain was stubbornly groggy and everything seemed muffled, muted even. *Which way is up? Which way is down?*

Sophie had turned into the wind.

She could not feel her body anywhere. And yet, there she still was, thinking those thoughts. *Why can't I wriggle my toes? Where are my hands?*

She was surging, moving forward. And she was not alone. She could feel herself being surrounded firmly by a strong, fierce gale. It was a vigorous tempest that gusted all around her. It cradled her, without there being touch; impelled her, without there being something that pushed. She felt she was caught in the eye of a storm, except that it was not calm and still and unmoving. A force unseen whisked her along – they were both vacillating and veering, but confidently, through the womb-like darkness that encapsulated them.

She imagined herself riding the fierce storm winds, surrendering to it as it careened and spiralled with her through the black void. At times, they both wrapped and folded into one another, intertwining into curves and curlicues and surging in the direction they were going. She arched into the deluge, trusting it, following it. There was nothing else in the moment but that dominating force that enveloped her and guided her and entwined her all at the same time. She forgot about her body. She forgot about seeing, hearing, smelling, tasting, feeling. All that mattered was the storm that encircled her.

For the first time in her life, Sophie felt completely safe, restful. She wanted the darkness to go on forever. She knew that nothing could harm her there. She was the wind, and she belonged to the storm.

Someone was calling her name.

Sophie.

Persephone.

The voice was low, intimate. She strained her ears to listen, but remembered that she had no ears.

Sophie, open your eyes. Sophie.

The voice grew larger and larger, filling up the theatre of her mind. It resonated in every corner and had a strange, gentle tugging quality to it. It was as though it had latched onto a loose end of her unravelling mind and was pulling it slowly, downward, downward, slowly, back down onto the ground.

Sophie could feel the darkness brightening around her, as though she had just awakened in the morning but had not yet opened her eyes. The sunrays filtered through her closed eyelids, suffusing the darkness with a warm glow.

Am I in my bed? Was I dreaming? Sophie wondered. She was afraid to open her eyes.

She knew that she had hands again, as someone took them both in his own. The man's hands were large and warm. She wanted to cry at the thought of having hands again, both with relief, and, oddly, with regret too. She held onto his hands with all her might, eyes still closed. They were starting to fill inexplicably with tears. She could not understand what she was feeling.

"Sophie, it's me. I'm here. Don't be afraid," it was Hades' voice.

Gradually, other parts of her body returned as well. She could feel her feet, standing on solid ground. Her heart was pounding erratically. There was a warm sensation, as she felt her face, her cheeks, her stomach. She was leaning, leaning against a man's chest.

He had pulled one hand free. Just as she was about to protest, the large warm hand moved to stroke her gently down her back. It was comforting. Sophie felt safe again. She could feel her breaths beginning to slow and her heart rate returning to normal. The man's hands moved to cradle the back of her head briefly before slowly moving her away and supporting her by her shoulders. She finally opened her eyes.

"Sophie, are you okay?" Hades peered down into her face.

On seeing his familiar kind eyes, Sophie started to cry again.

"I'm sorry!" she trembled. "I'm all out of sorts. Give me a moment, please."

Hades could not help himself. He embraced her again.

"Don't you worry about a thing. I'm here."

Sophie wrapped her arms around his waist and buried her face in the nape of his neck. He smelled like the cold air before an evening rain. She was afraid that she would fall if she let go. She had no idea what had transpired or where they were. She allowed herself to cry with abandon, to unburden her heart of the fear that gripped her.

Hades held her patiently. They stood there for a long time. Gradually, Sophie's sobs subsided from sheer exhaustion and she stepped back, hastily wiping her eyes with embarrassment.

"Where … where are we?" Sophie looked up at Hades, frightened to let her gaze leave his face. She did not know what she would see if she let herself look around.

"Sophie, we're in the Underworld. You, er, accidentally followed me here," Hades said, looking embarrassed himself.

She risked a small peek around her. They were standing in a vast meadow, carpeted in what looked to be *lalang* as tall as her waist.

"This is the Underworld?" Sophie asked, puzzled.

"Everyone sees it differently," Hades explained. "In fact, I don't even know what you are seeing."

"What do *you* see then?" Sophie looked back at him. She felt a smile growing despite herself.

"Right now?" Hades was looking at her intensely. "I'll tell you another time."

Sophie felt something snap in her mind. She had been lulled into a sense of unreality. The memories of what had transpired just moments ago at Mr Chang's house slammed back into her with all the force of a wayward truck. There was a hitch in her breath as she took in, *really* took in, what Hades had said.

"You mean to tell me that you brought me to the Underworld?" she exclaimed, a little more accusatorily than she intended.

"Well, you were the one who followed me here! I didn't do it on purpose!" Hades folded his arms. "I was simply going to … escort that escaped soul who had been tormenting Chang back here."

"You were going to … what?!?"

"That woman. Miss Lilac Peonies," Hades explained uncomplainingly. "She had been possessed by a soul of the dead who had somehow managed to escape the Underworld.

The soul had been using Chang to strengthen herself through having sex with him."

"Through having … what?!?"

"Sex," Hades said extremely patiently.

"I heard what you said. But *why*?!?"

"Well, I don't know! Perhaps I should ask my niece, Aphrodite, the next time I see her!"

"So, the reason Mr Chang was looking so peaky was because a ghost was … leaching his life force from him through having sex with him?"

"I suppose you could put it that way …"

Sophie felt an absurd urge to laugh but she quickly suppressed it. There were much more important matters at hand.

"Suppose I'm not dreaming right now, or hallucinating, or having a psychiatric breakdown … the reason you've brought the ghost tormenting Mr Chang back to the Underworld is because … you are Hades? As in, Hades, the ancient Greek God of the Underworld? *That* Hades?"

Hades folded his arms again. "Yes. I am."

"Have you always known? Were you lying to me about having amnesia then?"

"No!"

"Then, how do you know?"

"Know what?"

"That you are *that* Hades!"

Sophie was growing hysterical. She took a small step backward.

"Sophie. I swear, I did not go to the mortal realm to deceive you. I'm sorry I didn't immediately tell you the whole truth of who I am. In fact, I've only recently learned it myself. Or should I say, regained some sort of memory of what I am. There's a lot I need to tell you. But please give me some time. I'm still grappling with it myself."

He looked so morose that Sophie felt her heart yielding.

"Alright, alright," she patted him on the arm. "We'll talk another time."

"Do you remember that storybook? That fairy tale?"

"What fairy tale?"

"The one your mother said was your favourite as a little girl."

"What do you mean, my mother said? She talked to you?" Sophie was bewildered.

"Never mind that now. Do you remember the story?"

Sophie paused, thinking. It had been a long time since she had even cast a stray thought to her childhood storybooks.

"You mean *The Abduction of Persephone*? That story where the female character has the same name as I do," she finally replied. "I don't actually remember the details of the story. I just remember that pretty drawing of golden-haired Persephone on the cover of the book."

"Just for the record, I did not abduct you here, yeah? You *followed* me," Hades was glaring at her very seriously.

Sophie thought about it. "Yes, I suppose I did. I thought that ghost was gonna get you. And I wanted to push you out of the way. Or I suppose some reflex in me wanted to. So, I accidentally came here with you just at the moment you were pulling the ghost back down here. Where is she, anyway?"

Sophie looked around, suddenly remembering the horrifically distorted visage of poor Miss Lilac Peonies.

Hades harrumphed. "Did you think I'd let her hang around here like some delinquent? Cerberus took her back immediately."

"Cerberus?" Sophie brightened. "That's your dog!"

"Yes," Hades could not help it but allowed a broad grin to light up his face. "He's a good boy. Most of the time. I'd have to punish him for letting that soul escape, though. That was incredibly careless of him."

"No! Please, don't be too harsh on him. May I meet him? Please?"

At that, Hades grew solemn.

"Look, Sophie. I have to get you back before anyone notices. Come on."

"I still have so much to ask you! Do you really have a throne? Do you have a great big castle and piles of precious gems and treasures?"

"Come on! You're being a child. Let's go."

He took her hand. Sophie hesitated. She took one last look around the breathtaking meadow. It seemed to stretch on forever without bounds.

"How far does it go? Where is the horizon?" she said softly, shielding her eyes with one hand.

Hades' face was unreadable. "Close your eyes, Sophie."

~*~

Sophie had a hard time extricating herself from Hades' embrace after that second equally mercurial journey back. She felt strange, as though her fundamental particles had not been put back together quite right. There was something about him that would always be a part of her now. Trying to conceal her disappointment, Sophie straightened her clothes unnecessarily as Hades stepped away from her in a most insultingly perfunctory manner.

"Quick, I've got to get them both back into bed before they come to," Hades whispered. They were standing where they had been, right outside Mr Chang's door.

Sophie saw that Mr Chang had fainted. The two bodies were heaped in the hallway like corpses. She looked around nervously. It would be terribly awkward if someone were to walk in on them right now.

She tiptoed into the house behind Hades, shutting the door behind her. As she turned, she saw that Miss Lilac Peonies had been slung over Hades' shoulder. He was in the process of effortlessly lifting Mr Chang onto his other shoulder using his free arm.

"Guess you don't need my help then," she mumbled unnecessarily under her breath, following him as he carried the unconscious couple back into the bedroom.

She stared, marvelling at his otherworldly strength, as he arranged Mr Chang and Miss Lilac Peonies chastely side by side on the bed without breaking a sweat.

"Lord of the Underworld, huh?" she mused to herself softly. "You'd imagine more fire … and brimstone …"

"You're confusing it with the story of Satan and the Christian hell," Hades added nonchalantly, without looking up from his tasks.

Sophie blushed. "Oh, sorry. So, well, Lord of the Underworld, what are you doing here on earth then?"

Hades paused, glancing over at her. "Is it your wish that …

I return to where I belong?"

"No!" Sophie squeaked nervously. "No … I don't mean that. I'm just curious to know what it is you need here, on earth. Or, are you simply on vacation? I certainly don't begrudge that, no, good sir! Even the God of the Afterlife needs a break once in a while."

"I'm not on holiday," Hades replied curtly. "I'm here because I'm meant to be. But not because I wanted to. It's complicated. Can we talk another time?"

"Sure, sure," Sophie said hurriedly. "It's not so conducive to be discussing such portentous topics, whilst scurrying around like thieves in the dead of night."

She smiled at him tentatively.

Hades had finished his task of tucking the oblivious couple back into bed. He rounded the corner and stood facing Sophie.

"Sophie, I know that I owe you an explanation. Many explanations. You deserve as much, for all you have done for me. I'm sorry. I promise that I'll help you understand. Please trust me," he placed a hand on her shoulder.

Sophie nodded. "Let's go home."

~*~

Her blood grew cold as she unlatched the padlock and opened the door to her apartment. Someone was crying loudly from within.

"Mother!" Sophie gasped.

She thrust the padlock into Hades' hands and ran straight for her mother's bedroom.

She found Demeter curled up on the ground beside her bed, crying and groaning.

"Sophie … where are you, Sophie?" Demeter sobbed, her hands trembling. "I can't find my Sophie …"

"Mother! Shh, it's okay, I'm right here," Sophie knelt down next to the old lady, running her hands anxiously over her thin frame. "Does it hurt anywhere?"

She must have fallen while trying to get out of bed by herself in Sophie's absence. Tears of panic came to Sophie's eyes as she judiciously ran her fingers over her mother's joints, prodding gently.

There was a sharp intake of breath when she rubbed her mother's hipbones.

"It hurts, it hurts," she whispered.

"Here?" Sophie asked, her tears falling freely down her face now. "Don't worry, Mummy. I'll get you to the doctor's. He'll make it all better. Shh, now. It's okay."

She turned her head, not letting go of her mother's body, as she heard Hades enter the room.

"Would you call an ambulance, please?" she said as calmly as she could. "My mother's hurt. She must have fallen while trying to get out of bed."

Hades nodded, his face grave. "Leave it to me."

Sophie held her mother's trembling fingers and rested her forehead gently against hers.

"Just bear with it for a while, Mummy. Help is on the way. I'm here, now," she whispered.

The rest of the night flew by in a flurry of activity. Through it all, Sophie felt oddly numbed, as though she were operating on auto-pilot. She was glad for Hades' imperturbable strength, as he quietly and impassively took command of the emergency, supervising the paramedics as they transferred the old lady competently onto their stretcher and into the ambulance. She was glad for his light touch on the small of her back as they sat side by side in silence in the back of the ambulance. She was glad that he had guided her firmly by the elbow wordlessly through the bright lights and linoleum of the hospital to where she needed to be. She was glad that he sat beside her, solid and unmoving as a rock, letting her rest her head on his shoulder, as the emergency surgery stretched indeterminably for hours into the light of dawn.

He would have known the guilt that tore at her, the conviction that it was her fault for leaving her mother alone at home, but she wanted no consolation, no vapid words. And he offered none. At times, tears streamed unbidden down her face. She made no effort to wipe them away. She did not want him to look at her. And he did not.

At some point, Sophie must have fallen asleep, for she felt Hades shaking her awake.

"The surgery's over. We can go see your mother now," he said, peering into her eyes.

She could feel the warmth of his hand on her forearm. It reminded her of sunlight on wooden floorboards and Sunday afternoons. She was suddenly reluctant to get up, to move, to look her mother in the face. She felt so ashamed.

"Do you want to go see her now? You must be tired," Hades said. He was crouched in front of her and had both his hands on her forearms. His thumbs rubbed the insides of her elbows gently.

Sophie fought the urge to enfold herself in his embrace, to melt into his strength and to hide away like a child. She stood up.

"Yes, I want to see her," she said slowly.

They stood outside the glass window of the ward for a long time. Sophie's mother was fast asleep. The nurses had reassured them that the operation went well and that she would recover in time. Sophie watched dazedly as the machines beeped her vitals monotonously. She gazed at the taped needle that punctured the delicate skin on the back of her mother's hand. It had already started to bruise.

"I'll come back again tonight," she announced to no one in particular.

She started a little as Hades placed a hand atop her head and smoothed her hair down in small languid strokes.

"Your hair is very messy," he informed her.

Sophie started to smile a little, despite herself. Self-consciously, she brushed her hair behind her ears.

"I'll come back with you tonight, too. Let's go home for now," Hades had removed his hand from her hair. It was now stretched out in front of her, palm up, a question in his eyes.

She slipped her own hand into his and closed it tight, answering it.

1 THE FIRE TRUCK AND THE POMEGRANATE

Sophie closed the flower shop for two weeks and spent all her time with her convalescing mother.

"Does it hurt anywhere, Mummy?" her heart ached at the sight of her mother, so pale and wan against the stark white of the hospital bed.

"What is it, Sophie? What hurts?" her mother replied weakly, raising a hand to Sophie's face.

Sophie rushed to hold her hand. At least the painkillers were doing their job. She breathed a sigh of relief.

"Sophie, did you fall down again? Did you take the training wheels off your bicycle already?" her mother said hoarsely, smiling faintly at her.

"Yes, Mummy, I can ride the bicycle so well now," Sophie replied, framing her own cheek with her mother's hand. "You should see me sometime, Mama. I can go so fast."

"Sophie, you have to be careful when you play outside, okay?"

"Okay, Mama. I promise to be careful."

The doctor had informed Sophie that her mother had broken her right hip, but with enough bedrest, she would recover well with no major complications. Sophie sighed again as she watched her mother's eyelids drifting shut. She slipped in and out of a light sleep from day to day. Sophie hoped her mother would regain enough strength soon, at least to be wheeled outside into the garden.

She was so deep in her reverie she barely noticed a hand alighting on the back of her chair.

"I come bearing nourishment," Hades announced, placing the little bag of takeaway food on the small table at the foot of the hospital bed.

He peered into Sophie's face. "You have to take care of yourself, boss. My livelihood depends on you, you know?"

Sophie was glad to see him. "From delivering bouquets to delivering food now, huh? I'm sorry. This was not what you signed up for."

"You'll be back to work soon, when Aunty recovers. For now, I accept the ad hoc modifications to my professional duties with absolutely no complaints."

Sophie felt her heart lighten. She wanted to reach out for his hand, but stopped herself. She had let herself grow careless that last time, leaving her mother at home alone just to follow Hades. The guilt lingered malodorously, wafting over her leeringly every time she wanted to let herself drift close to Hades. She felt so stupid, so angry at herself. On hindsight, she was amazed at how irresponsible she had been. She knew that in her mother's condition, simply attempting to get out of bed by herself was dangerous. And yet she had chosen to ignore the risk. She hated herself. She felt her mother's pain as her own. It was so tempting, so easy, to fall and to let Hades catch her. To have someone take care of her for once. To forget all her responsibilities as a caregiver and to do whatever her heart desired. But she forbade herself from seeking comfort. She did not deserve it. There was a penance she had to pay, at least for the moment.

If Hades was frustrated at her careful distance, he did not show it. He treated her with respect and compassion, and simply looked out for her in that light-hearted, casual manner she was so grateful for.

"The food is getting cold," he urged her.

Hades strode over to her and picked up her chair with her still in it, and carried it nonchalantly over to the table. She could not help but squeal a little, only to quickly suppress it so as not to disturb the other patients in the ward. Hades appeared oblivious to the few bemused stares directed their way, paying attention only to Sophie.

"Hades!" Sophie whispered. "People are looking at us."

"Sophie!" Hades whispered back, mimicking her outraged tone. "You deserve it, for being such a naughty girl. Now, be good and eat your dinner."

Sophie looked into his eyes. Her heart ached to see the soft tenderness she found there. She suddenly remembered the picture she had taken of him with her phone. It seemed like such a long time ago. She had grown to know those eyes a lot better now. There was so much she wanted to say to him, and so much she wanted to know about him. But the narrow hospital bed was wide as a valley between them, a chasm that she could not yet bring herself to cross.

Nevertheless, he was right there beside her, smiling ruefully down at her. And that was good enough.

~*~

Sophie soon grew to terribly miss her well-ordered world. Once her mother was given the green light by her doctor to resume convalescence at home, Sophie gratefully enlisted the help of Hanna once more and returned to the sanctuary that was her flower shop.

It was Thursday, an odd day of the week to resume operations, but she relished it all the same. As Sophie slipped on her familiar apron and into the routine flow of her chores, she felt herself remembering how to breathe again. The scent of dried flowers in the shop embraced her like an old friend. Her neatly-labelled jars of floral tea were lined up as vigilantly as a platoon of soldiers at her command. The bamboo wind chime aptly preceded her own effervescent welcome to customers.

She was regretful of having to throw away a substantial number of wilted flowers, but cheered up at the thought of Hades coming back from the wholesaler with new batches. It was a fresh start. She was eager and ready to get back to work.

It was mid-afternoon when a woman came into the shop. Sophie thought she had never seen anyone look so dejected. Approximating her to be in her early thirties, the customer was dressed plainly, like a school teacher, and had her long black hair tied into a single plait that trailed down her back. She had good-looking, refined features that would have been extremely attractive if she did not look so utterly distraught. Sophie's chest contracted with sympathy.

"Good afternoon, Ma'am. How can I help you today?" she smiled gently, keeping her voice soft and even. "Do have a seat. I was just about to make some rosebud white tea. Would you care to join me?"

The lady adjusted her shoulder bag nervously. She looked around, unsure of herself.

"Come, I'm sure you can tell me what you need over a cup of tea," Sophie had breezily pulled out one of her favourite English-styled tea sets, consisting of a powder-blue rounded pot delicately dotted with roses and two matching sets of cups and saucers.

Feeling herself relent in Sophie's unflappable sweet temper, the lady climbed up onto a stool and put her shoulder bag down on the one next to her.

"It smells lovely," she said docilely, as they both watched the mist rise from the spout.

"It does, doesn't it? Floral teas always put me in a mellow mood."

"You seem really passionate about all things floral," a tiny smile had emerged on the woman's face.

"There's something about beauty that is good and true, don't you think?" Sophie poured the tea slowly. "We turn to beautiful things when our hearts are aching."

The woman watched the tea introspectively. Sophie's small delicate movements lulled her into an inexplicable sense of peace.

When she looked up again, Sophie saw that tears had sprung to her eyes.

"I'm so sorry! I don't know what's gotten into me," the woman apologised profusely, rushing to extricate a packet of tissues from her bag.

"It's quite alright. I understand that some days are … difficult. I've been going through somewhat of a rough patch myself. We just have to try to keep going on, right?" Sophie touched the woman's arm briefly in solidarity. "Come, warm your stomach and warm your heart."

She slid a cup of tea across the counter. The golden liquid quivered, catching the light. A dash of small purple petals floated serenely on its surface.

The woman dabbed at her eyes with a piece of tissue and took a sip from the dainty teacup.

"It's so fragrant!" she exclaimed. The cup was so beautiful, serving as a soothing backdrop to the showiness of the rosebud tea.

"I have my secret blend," Sophie winked, raising her own cup to her lips.

"Thank you so much for this," the woman said. She stuck out a hand. "My name is Anne. It's really nice to meet you."

"Likewise! I'm Sophie."

Sophie's hand was warm from handling the tea. Anne smiled.

"You have a really nice place here. I don't think I've ever been in a flower shop like this," she said, looking around more restfully this time.

"Thank you! You're too kind," Sophie beamed. "By the way, who is it you're buying flowers for? May I know what the occasion is? I can help you create a bespoke bouquet, specially tailored for your needs."

Anne hesitated. She took a deep breath and started rummaging around her roomy shoulder bag. Finally, she fished out a small toy fire truck.

"I'm glad to hear you say that. I have been wondering if it would be too much of a hassle to ask. Would you be able to make me a bouquet of flowers incorporating this little fire truck?"

"Sure, I can!" Sophie chirped. She took the toy from Anne courteously. "It's so adorable."

"My son loves ... loved ... fire trucks of all kinds. He was always clamouring for me to buy him more. I mean, they all look so similar, don't they? I can never tell them apart."

Sophie did not miss her correction to past tense. Her heart constricted.

"There are some with ladders, like this one does. And then there are the ... smaller ones ... for the advance party of firefighters, he said ... those ... seat only ... four ..." Anne's words were breaking apart and dissolving into small sobs she desperately tried to swallow.

Sophie lifted the latched opening and came around to stand by Anne's shoulder. She placed a hand on her back and rubbed it softly as Anne started crying in earnest, her tears flowing in an unstoppable deluge.

"I'm sorry! I'm so embarrassed," Anne buried her face in her hands. The tissue paper she held was disintegrating rapidly into damp shreds.

Sophie fetched her a new piece of tissue, and pinched the little damp shreds away from Anne's fingers. The sight of the tiny soggy pieces suddenly looked incredibly funny and absurd. The piece of tissue had become pathetic and helpless in the flood of Anne's tears. Both women started laughing a little, and then relentlessly, in hysterical waves.

Sophie patted Anne's shoulder softly and ducked back under the counter to throw the wet tissue pieces away.

"Today's the first anniversary of my son's death. His name was Benton. He was only six years old. He dreamt of becoming a firefighter. It was all he talked about," Anne said, twisting her replacement tissue paper round and round her index finger. "I'm going to visit his gravestone for the first time. Back then, I just … couldn't do it. It took me months to truly come to terms with it. To believe that he is gone from me forever."

Sophie stroked the little fire truck. She could not find the words to express the pain she felt. Impulsively, she reached across the counter and simply held Anne's hand tightly.

"I'll make him the best goddamned fire truck bouquet in the world," she declared.

Anne squeezed her hand back.

~*~

Sophie's hands worked at lightning speed. This time, she very quickly formed a vivid image in her mind of what she wanted to create. She used bright orange hibiscus as the focal flowers, and added wide extravagant tropical leaves to create an explosive, firework effect. She then added a few stalks of crimson calla lilies as accents, and to bring the red of the toy fire truck into the composition. She arranged the riot of a bouquet into an inconspicuous but sturdy, low square vase so it could stand on its own without requiring external support.

"Sophie, that is simply marvelous," Anne gasped when she saw the finished product. "It's so beautiful. I can't believe it."

"I did my best for Benton," Sophie said simply.

It was a particularly bulky piece. Sophie contemplated it for a moment, and looked at the clock on the wall.

"Do you mind waiting? My colleague will be back soon, and he would be able to help you with this. He does all my deliveries," Sophie explained.

"Oh, but I'm heading there right now myself," Anne replied.

"It's going to be hard to carry that on your own, especially with that huge bag you already have there! Will you wait? He won't be long," Sophie smiled.

"Alright, that sounds like a good idea. Don't worry, I'll pay for the delivery service."

"Well, since you offered to … I shan't stand on ceremony," Sophie teased.

Anne grew serious. "Sophie, thank you for all that you've done. You don't know how much this means to me. I'm so glad that of all florists, I found you. I only wish that Benton could see this beautiful piece for himself."

She gazed at the bright, cheerful explosion of flower and foliage that stood so self-assuredly on the counter, as though proud of how much space it took up.

Sophie was pensive. "I wish too that I could take it to him. And tell him how much his mama loves him, and will always remember him for as long as she lives."

The women locked eyes for a second. They both contemplated the bittersweet grief that inevitably came with the condition of being alive.

The wind chime sounded, breaking their reverie. The deliveryman had returned.

~*~

Sophie could not stop thinking about Anne and Benton. For days after that, she found herself staring into space, envisioning the fire truck bouquet she had made. She thought of the little boy who would never grow up to become a firefighter. She thought of the *lalang* fields of the Underworld. Was he waiting for Anne in the afterworld? Was he afraid? Was he lonely? Was he at peace? Did he miss his mother?

"What is it, Sophie?" Hades demanded, waving a dish cloth in front of her face. "Will you tell me what's bothering you? It's killing me."

"What?" Sophie turned, puzzled.

"I can tell that you've been fretting over something for days. Will you please talk to me about it? I'm dying to know. I want to help."

"Oh," Sophie intoned. She frowned. "I don't really know how to say it."

"It's okay. Try me. If you sound crazy, I promise I'll pretend I never heard anything."

"Okay," Sophie said, and told him everything she was thinking about. She told him about her afternoon with Anne, whom he had accompanied to the cemetery with the fire truck bouquet. She told him of her wish to give the bouquet to little Benton herself and to tell him that he was loved. She wanted to see for herself how Benton was doing. She wanted … to let Anne know that Benton was waiting happily for her until the time came for her to join him in the afterlife. She wanted Anne to know that Benton was in a beautiful place.

"Is he?" Sophie asked, turning her eyes to Hades beseechingly. "Is he in the beautiful part of your Underworld? Is he at peace?"

Hades put the dish cloth down and sighed heavily.

"First, I can't answer that because I don't have the register of all the souls of the dead in the world memorised in my head. Second, are you certain of what you are asking for? To go back there again?"

Sophie nodded vigorously. "Yes, I want to go there. It's your domain, your kingdom, isn't it? You are the master and commander of the Underworld, after all. Will you then authorise me for a short visit, please?"

Hades stared hard at her. "The Underworld is not some tourist destination."

"I know it's a lot to ask," Sophie admitted. "I know it's … frivolous of me to even suggest it. Look, forget it. I'm sorry I asked."

"Argh! How can I fight that?!?" Hades mock-shielded his eyes.

"What is it?" Sophie cried.

"Those eyes of yours," Hades said grudgingly.

"No, Hades, I don't mean it! I … I don't want to ask the impossible. I'm really sorry. Please just forget that I said anything."

"Excuse me? The impossible? As you said so yourself, I *am* lord and master of the Underworld," Hades narrowed his brows.

"So you will take me then? Just a quick visit. In and out. Nobody will find out," Sophie could barely contain her excitement.

"Why should I be concerned if anyone finds out? I don't need anyone's permission to come and go as I please," Hades looked mildly insulted.

"You're right, you're right! It's your empire after all! You are the ultimate authority!" Sophie said brightly, grinning from ear to ear. "Come on, hurry, we gotta get to the cemetery first!"

"What?"

"The fire truck bouquet! Were you listening before? Come on, quick!"

"It's a lot more hassle to get to the cemetery than to the Underworld," Hades grumbled unhappily, taking off his apron and hanging it neatly on its usual place.

"Stop complaining and let's go! We've got to get back in time for the end of Hanna's shift," Sophie said, pushing him out of the door.

"Not only are you demanding me to take you to *my* domain to visit the soul of a boy you don't know, you are also *rushing* me?"

"I didn't *demand* for you to take me," Sophie said patiently. "I asked you so nicely. *You're* the one who said that you didn't need anyone's permission to take me there."

"You bet I don't need anyone's permission."

"Yes, alright, quick, let's go."

~*~

Sophie held the fire truck bouquet in both hands. It still looked lively and presentable. She hesitated.

"Er, Hades," she said sweetly. "Would this be … squished? Do you promise to get it there nicely in one piece?"

"I got *you* there in one piece and back, didn't I? *You*, a whole person!" Hades exploded with exasperation.

"Okay, okay," Sophie said placatingly and stepped closer to him. She felt a little shy to know what was coming.

Hades stood behind her and wrapped his arms around her, his palms resting against hers on the vase.

And they turned into the wind.

~*~

Sophie rejoiced to see the peaceful *lalang* field again. The feathery white grasses caressed her knees teasingly, as though welcoming her back. They extended as far as the eye could see. The sky was cloudless and modestly azure, coyly retreating from attention. Strands of her hair started dancing happily in the balmy air as Sophie turned round and round, trying to soak up as much as she could.

Hades watched her with amusement. He was glad she enjoyed his waiting room. He called up a console that resembled a sleek computer screen, mounted at comfortable eye level on a slim brushed silver stand.

"Oh wow! Is that how you access the register of all souls?"

"Why are you so impressed? I learned it from the mortals after all," Hades shrugged. "Most processes here are already automated. I hardly have to do anything at all."

"You mean you outsourced the judgment of mortal souls to computer algorithms?" Sophie asked accusatorily.

"Algorithms that *I* wrote myself, following *my* rules and *my* principles," Hades retorted pointedly.

"Oh. So the computer sorts the souls for you according to set criteria and assigns them their final destination in the Underworld. How convenient! I suppose that makes a lot more sense than for you to assess them one by one."

"Well, I still have to personally deal with the *appeals*," Hades added darkly. "That keeps me busy enough. I also make the rounds to make sure that the souls are sorted correctly. There are still bound to be errors from time to time."

Before Sophie could ask even more questions about the topography of the Underworld, he quickly turned back to the console and entered the boy's name.

"Ah, there he is," Hades smiled, relieved.

"Where is he? Let's go see him, please!"

"He's in the Elysian Fields."

Sophie felt she could jump for joy. But she tightened her grip around her fire truck bouquet. "I'm glad to hear that. Is it far from here?"

"Not when you're with me," Hades replied.

He grabbed her arm and, then, they arrived.

Sophie blinked.

It was as though she had merely been standing in a projected hologram, which then transformed in a second to show a different landscape. The first thing she noticed were the distant rolling hills, ambling mistily along the horizon and rising gradually into mountains that peeked far beyond sight. A fast-flowing freshwater stream sang and gurgled behind her, extending into the mouth of a forest. It looked dense and inviting. The smell of pine and birch filled the air. She gasped as she took a step, breaking a small branch hidden beneath the damp moss underfoot.

They stood in front of a small red and yellow timber house, cool in the shade of an enormous tree. Beyond it, Sophie could just about make out miles of untouched wilderness, sprawling lazily beneath the slate-grey sky.

Just then, a small rag-tag group of boisterous children spilled out from within the belly of the forest. They were gambolling in high spirits, many holding onto baskets filled with blueberries and mushrooms. Sophie recognised Benton immediately from the picture of him she had seen on his gravestone. He had a mop of unruly hair and purple blueberry stains on one cheek. Breaking off from a joke he was telling his friends, the little boy turned and looked towards where Sophie and Hades stood waiting.

As he came nearer and nearer, Sophie could see his gaze flitting to the vibrant bouquet she held in her hands, from which the little toy fire truck peeked out prominently. She knelt down to match his height and gazed into his eyes.

"Benton," she called softly. "My name is Sophie. I come from the world of the living, with a gift from your mother."

She held the bouquet out to him with some trepidation.

To her relief, Benton lit up with delight as he received the gift from Sophie. His small fingers shot to the little toy fire truck immediately, gleeful and admiring.

"This is from my mummy?" he asked Sophie, averting his gaze shyly in the manner of children meeting a stranger for the first time.

"Yes, from your mummy, Anne. She has become a friend of mine," Sophie continued encouragingly. "She asked me to make this specially for you. And to tell you that she loves you and misses you very much."

"Will she be coming for me soon?" Benton mumbled, studiously fixing his gaze on the bouquet rather than on Sophie. "I miss my mummy."

"Yes, she will come for you," Sophie said. "Wait for her here, Benton. Before you know it, she will be with you again and live with you happily forever."

"Live with me here?" Benton's eyes shone with enchantment. "I want her to! I want to teach her how to pick the blueberries in the forest ... and to follow the river into a special ... cave ... full of treasures ... I want to show her ... everything!"

In his excitement, he stumbled over the words that poured from him faster than he could keep up with. At the same time, he patted the toy fire truck nestled in the bouquet.

"Mummy bought me this fire truck?" he finally met Sophie's eyes falteringly.

"Yes, she did."

"Will she come to play with it with me?"

"Yes, she will."

"Soon?"

"Yes, Benton. Will you be a good boy and wait for her?"

"I will wait right here," Benton broke into a toothy grin.

Sophie felt her calves starting to cramp. She stood up and looked around for Hades. He was crouched by the lake, leisurely inspecting a population of nettles.

"I'm going home now," she said to Benton. "Thanks for talking to me today."

Benton hugged the bouquet to his chest, suddenly unsure. He reached for a corner of Sophie's skirt.

"You are Mummy's friend?" he asked hesitantly.

"Yes, I am."

"Will you … will you … tell her that Benton loves Mummy?" he stumbled hurriedly.

With that, he turned and ran towards the red and yellow house. The riotous bouquet spread widely beyond his silhouette on both sides like fiery wings.

Sophie watched him go. Her heart ached and she felt like crying. What seemed like such a good idea before left her with a pain that lingered stubbornly in her chest. She felt a little foolish and very confused. She did not think that she had achieved anything at all by coming here.

Sighing, she sat down on a stray boulder in the garden. She could hear shrieks of laughter from the children in the house. There were fruit trees all around, abundant and lush, and full of jutting, enticing branches that begged to be climbed by small hands and feet. Benton was happy and at peace in the Elysian Fields.

But what did she wish to achieve by telling Anne anything about the Underworld? Would the knowledge spur Anne to in fact take her own life? And if she did, would she be able to reach the Elysian Fields? Was it an act that would tilt the scales and send her somewhere else instead, say, the Fields of Mourning or the Asphodel Meadows? If Sophie instructed her to live a good, virtuous life, would she then fall into worry and obsession over what counts as a life worth a place in the

Elysian Fields? As it turned out, Sophie could not tell Anne anything at all.

Hades ambled unhurriedly to where Sophie fretted. He took in her silence, her deep contemplation.

"Let's go home," he said.

Sophie raised her eyes. "I'm sorry, Hades. I should have thought this through."

"So, you understand," Hades said simply.

"I do."

They lapsed into a momentary silence. Sunlight dappled through the trees. A playful breeze tickled and agitated their leaves.

Suddenly remembering something, Sophie smiled to herself.

"Doesn't that old story have Hades giving Persephone a pomegranate to eat? Now that I've thought of it, I do feel rather hungry."

"It depends on which version you are referring to," Hades said lightly. "The one I've heard merely involves some nondescript gardener, and not the Lord of the Underworld himself."

"Is it true then? That if I eat something from the Underworld, I would be bound here forever?"

"No," Hades said. "It's not true."

"How can you prove it?" Sophie teased.

"Well, you can eat a damned pomegranate and go back to where you belong. Is that the scientific experiment you are looking for?"

"Hmm," Sophie mused, gazing at Hades. He appeared to be avoiding her eyes. "I think you're tricking me. You want me to eat the pomegranate, just like in the story, so I will belong to you forever."

"If it were only so easy!" Hades exclaimed, exasperated.

"Your realm, your rules, right?"

"Well, what if I don't want to? What if I don't want to decree that eating a fruit from the Underworld binds you here forever? What if that's not the way I want to …" he trailed off.

"Want to what?" Sophie egged him on, her eyes glistening.

"You know. You're just making me say it."

"Yes, I want to hear you say it."

Hades frowned unhappily at Sophie. "Why must you make things so explicit?"

"Are you embarrassed?" Sophie goaded him.

Hades glared at her. For the first time, he faked a cough and looked away.

Sophie moved closer to him. She prodded him insistently with one finger.

"Finish your sentence, please," she said.

Hades looked back to her and sighed ostentatiously.

"That's not the way I want you to be with me," he mumbled incoherently.

"What?"

"I don't wish to compel you, or force you, or make you do anything you don't want to do, alright? I don't want you to be with me just because you ate a damned fruit."

"I want it," Sophie proclaimed. "Please give me a pomegranate."

"Pick it yourself," Hades replied grumpily. "There are tons over there."

"No, I want you to give it to me. As a gift. I don't want to *steal* from the Underworld."

"It's not stealing if I'm giving you permission."

"But I want you to give me a present!"

Hades glared at Sophie, maddened with inexplicable emotions. His eyes darkened and he pulled Sophie roughly to him. Raising her chin with his fingers, he bent his head and kissed her.

Sophie froze for a second. She felt his arms circle around her, pulling her into him, closer and closer and closer. His lips on hers were warm with sunshine. She kissed him back, resolutely, defiantly. She clutched the hair at the back of his head and pushed herself up against him.

Hades broke away first. Sophie peeked at his eyes, still overcast with desire. He stood up from their boulder and went to the nearest short, stumpy tree. He yanked a single pomegranate from the tree and returned to Sophie.

He held it out to her. The taut skin of the ripe fruit was a deep lustrous scarlet. Sophie took it from him. She examined it from every angle. It looked just like any mortal pomegranate. There was nothing unworldly about it. She rolled it around her hands uncertainly, not knowing what to do with it.

"Hades, this is embarrassing, but I've never actually eaten a pomegranate before," she laughed. "How do I cut it open? I don't have a knife with me."

Hades snatched the fruit back from her and broke it apart with his bare hands. The unctuous, secret red seeds burst forth from its fibrous constraints and glimmered lavishly in the sun.

"Show off," Sophie muttered.

Not looking away from him, she scooped a handful of the dewy red seeds with her fingers and slipped them into her mouth, one at a time. Hades watched as the small slippery kernels reddened her lips. Juice dripped messily from Sophie's hand, but she paid it no heed. She continued to glide the pomegranate seeds casually into her mouth, closing her eyes as the sweetness exploded on her tongue. As the small heap on her hand diminished and disappeared, she leisurely licked her fingers clean of the pomegranate juice.

"That was delicious. Thank you," Sophie said courteously.

"You're welcome. And now, I'll take you home."

Sophie paused. *This is your home,* she thought. *One day, you'll have to come back here again, to resume your rule over the souls of the dead.*

But she did not want to ask him when. At the moment, she could not bear the thought of being apart from him. And so, without saying a word, she stepped once more into his arms.

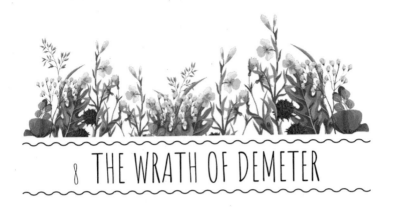

8 THE WRATH OF DEMETER

The days passed languidly. Sophie and Hades let themselves be lulled into a seemingly indefinite game of playing house. They worked, broke bread and journeyed back and forth to the flower shop together. The stolen kisses and meaningful glances did not escape Demeter's attention. Angered by the love that grew between them, she decided that it was time for her to act. As the advent of technology gave humanity command and control over nature, the Goddess of the Harvest no longer played a significant role in human affairs. But she was still a goddess after all, and the uneasy relationship that mortals had with nature was easy enough for her to exploit.

It was no more than the softest push that induced the fall of dominoes. As humanity extended their reach deeper and wider into the remaining wilderness, so did their exposure to new strains of zoonotic viruses. The gentle push and pull of chance warred invisibly every minute and every second, naked to the human eye … Just one quirk of statistical probability, and there … there was the tiniest of genetic mutations that allowed the jump of a new, deadly infectious disease from beast to man. This time, Demeter simply watched, cold-eyed. She did nothing as it spread unfettered across the globe, unlike the many, *many* other times in which she had intervened, out of pity and compassion for the mortals that she had looked out for over the centuries.

I'll send them all to you this time, Lord of the Underworld.

~*~

Hades frowned as he found an unmarked envelope on the desk in his bedroom. It was not there when he had left for work in the morning. He removed the sheath of paper from within and unfolded it. It was a letter, addressed to him:

Dear Lord of the Underworld Esteemed Hades the Righteous King of Darkness,

I hope this letter finds you well. This is Hermes, Herald of the Gods, and not to mention, the God of Trade, Wealth, Luck, Fertility, Animal Husbandry, Sleep, Language, Thieves and Travel His Good Self. I hope you forgive me for not seeking you out in person, for I am currently working remotely. (It has increased my productivity by 200%!)

I trust that on your long sojourn in the mortal realm, you have come to be aware of the new infectious disease sweeping the globe. I speak on behalf of the Good and the All-Powerful Olympian Gods in condemning this disruptive and unnecessary phenomenon presently sowing discord and disorder in the mortal world.

Upon thorough investigation by the Emergency Task Force formed by My Good Self, the God of Trade, Wealth, Luck, Fertility, Animal Husbandry, Sleep, Language, Thieves and Travel, I have come to the irrefutable conclusion that this infectious disease pandemic has been wrought upon the mortal realm by none other than Demeter, the Goddess of the Harvest.

Upon the appraisal of the Good and the All-Powerful Olympian Gods, it is to our Utter and Utmost Dismay to understand that the pandemic is a mere Act of Vengeance enacted upon Your Good Self the Lord of the Underworld Esteemed Hades the Righteous King of Darkness.

Please consider yourself duly informed that the uncharacteristic influx of souls entering the Underworld in such a short period of time has overwhelmed the processing capabilities of your lieutenants, The Three Judges of the Dead, King Minos, Aeacus and Rhadamanthus. In fact, a backlog of unprocessed souls has leaked through to the oceans and seas, polluting the marine life through Unlawful Spiritual Possession, and, as a result, gravely inconvenienced your Furious and Wrathful brother, Poseidon, Great God of the Sea, Earthquakes, Storms and Horses.

On official decree of the Supreme and All-Mighty Zeus, God of the Sky and Thunder, and King of the Good and the All-Powerful Olympian Gods, you are hereby summoned for a hearing on the basis of Dereliction of Duty and Gross Negligence. It shall also be attended by Demeter, Goddess of the Harvest, facing one count of the charge of Abuse of Authority.

Should you have any queries requiring my physical presence in the mortal realm, kindly supply the usual libation of nectar, milk and sweet wine, topped off with a splash of tonic water and white barley.

Yours sincerely,
Hermes
Herald of the Gods,
The God of Trade, Wealth,
Luck, Fertility, Animal Husbandry,
Sleep, Language, Thieves and Travel.

Hades put the letter down and pinched the bridge of his nose. He had not guessed that Demeter was behind the raging pandemic that had taken so many mortal lives. He supposed he had let himself grow complacent and unguarded. It was, indeed, most irresponsible of him. Still, he was taken aback at the utter lengths to which Demeter would go to just to get back at him. Or perhaps she was simply creating a diversion to force him to return to the Underworld. Whichever it was, she was certainly successful. In only nine months, the new infectious disease had claimed more than a million mortal lives across the world. Hades had not thought of the toll it would have taken on Minos, Aeacus and Rhadamanthus. He made up his mind to raise their annual performance bonuses when he returned.

Hades re-read Hermes' letter, flipping through it several times. For such a long-winded letter, that accursed messenger of the gods had forgotten to indicate the date and time of the trial. Hades had to summon him to the mortal realm to provide further clarifications after all.

Mightily annoyed, Hades put on a surgical face mask and set off for the nearest supermarket to buy the requisite ingredients to summon Hermes. He hoped he could restrain himself from strangling Hermes when he showed up. Every god he knew avoided that irritating, self-important prick as much as they could. He had grown even more infuriatingly narcissistic ever since he discovered the luxury haute couture brand named after him. Hermes religiously followed every season's menswear collection and delighted in decking himself out in the latest mortal fashions.

Having bought the necessary ingredients, Hades parked himself at one of the old blue-and-white tiled chess tables, complete with matching seats, at the void deck of a public housing block. It was fairly deserted at that time of night. Irritably, he fished out a paper plate from his grocery bag and placed it on the table. In the Underworld, his ruling jurisdiction, he would have been able to summon Hermes with the snap of a finger. But this was the mortal realm, and there were troublesome procedures to be followed. It irked him immensely to have to perform the ritual like any other mere mortal. He could already imagine Hermes' insufferably smug grin.

Hades rooted around the grocery bag and brought out the bottle labelled '100% Pure, Raw, Unfiltered, Organic Manuka Honey'. Not bothering with aesthetics, he uncapped the squeezy bottle and unceremoniously squirted a few generous splashes onto the paper plate. Next came the small carton of milk, uncapped and dribbled into the mix. *Ah,* the next one he would be sure to keep for himself as a treat afterward. It was an expensive vintage dessert wine of a reputable brand. Hades unscrewed the top and poured the tiniest amount possible onto the concoction. Finally, a splash of tonic water and a heap of white barley. Hades poured the entire can of barley seeds onto the plate, letting them soak up the other liquids.

"Hermes, Herald of the Gods, I summon thee," Hades muttered, putting away the assorted containers back into the grocery bag desultorily.

There was a brief ripple in the still, humid air. A fashionably gaunt, lanky man turned the corner and loped insouciantly towards where Hades sat. Hermes had his hair styled in the tight curls that were currently *de rigeur* in men's fashion magazines. His heavy brows, carefully groomed and shaped with tweezers, framed his ancient yet perpetually mischievous eyes. Hades wondered where on the globe he had arrived from; he was certainly not dressed for Singapore's humid weather. Hermes sported a dark maroon shirt with a matching varsity-style jacket over pale pink pants, grey athleisure-chic sandals, a bright orange scarf around his neck. It sat loosely around his prominent, jutting Adam's apple, accentuating the angles of his jaw, which were still proudly visible despite the mandatory face mask he also wore.

"For heaven's sake. You look like a court jester," Hades curled a corner of his lip to show his distaste.

"Says the guy who possesses not the least shred of aesthetic sensibility," Hermes retorted amiably. "You would not recognise art if it slapped you in the face."

"True art does not *slap*," Hades replied drily. "You would proclaim a heap of horse dung an instantiation of the sublime if it suited the season."

"Horse dung? Court jester? Come on. Your insults are truly as dated as that sad outfit of yours ... which kind of screams toxic masculinity, by the way. Not a good look in the twenty-first century, IMHO," Hermes replied, not bothering to explain the acronym.

"What's toxic is your wretched attempt to keep up with the vagaries of mortal fashions. Please, don't debase yourself so. It's embarrassing to watch."

"Communications is my domain expertise," Hermes shrugged. "It's practically in my job description to stay current.

It's hard work, you know? I've just come from a seminar on digital marketing in Berlin."

"Don't think I don't know that all conferences have been moved online nowadays," Hades rolled his eyes. "A seminar in the middle of a pandemic? Don't make me laugh."

"Well, fine, a webinar. And I *was* attending said webinar in my apartment in Berlin. You should come visit sometime, after this whole mess is over. Which reminds me!" Hermes' eyes gleamed wickedly. "The mess that *you* are partly responsible for. Ugh! Don't you feel any guilt in putting the mortals through this?"

"How dare you?" Hades roared. "It is *not* my fault that this happened."

"Yes, it is," Hermes stuck out his tongue childishly. "You busy being all lovey-dovey with your new girlfriend while her jealous mother wrecks disaster upon the world!"

"Humanity brought this situation upon themselves. We have nothing to do with it," Hades said curtly.

"Well … I suppose the humans did spurn Demeter when they took the matters of agriculture into their own hands … I hear they even use machine learning and data analytics to perfect the art of the harvest these days."

"Nobody knows Demeter anymore. They no longer erect temples in her name nor make any offerings to her. She has long been absolved of any responsibilities as Goddess of the Harvest."

"Not true. No one but Zeus himself has the authority to excuse the gods and goddesses from their duties. As far as we all know, she is still a goddess and presides over grain and fertility of the earth. It doesn't matter how much or how little the human beings need her. A duty is a duty. And she has abused her powers as Goddess of the Harvest in triggering this pandemic."

"Did she, really?" Hades was keenly curious.

"According to my investigations into the origins of the new infectious disease, it is highly likely that she was involved. Hence, the trial. You understand how these things go."

"Yes, the trial! For all your braggadocious communications expertise, you forgot to indicate the date, time and place of the trial in your letter," Hades said pointedly.

"Aha! Now who's the one who has been picking up bad habits from the humans?" Hermes punched the air with a triumphant finger. "It must have been too long since you received a summons from Zeus. When he wants to see us, it means, uh, *immediately*."

"Is he in Mount Olympus now? If I were to journey there and find that he's not even there, you will be …" Hades made a strangling motion with his hands.

Hermes suddenly seemed unsure. "Oh yes," he admitted. "Zeus has vacation homes in every single continent on earth. And not to mention those for all his mistresses, too. Right, he, er, might not *necessarily* be at Mount Olympus at the moment, per se."

"Ha! So, someone has not done his due diligence after all. You mean for Demeter and I to wait around aimlessly on Mount Olympus while you traipse the globe looking for Zeus? Further exacerbating my alleged *dereliction of duties*?" Hades glared at him witheringly.

"Ah," Hermes said. "Yes, it seems that my event management skills are not up to scratch after all. I shall have to take a MOOC on that."

Hades did not bother to ask him to explain this other new acronym. "So, do your job then. Time, place, venue. I'll be awaiting your *kind follow up.*"

Just then, a pair of police officers approached them. They were dressed rather casually, in white polo T-shirts bearing the Singapore Police Force crest, and what appeared to be black bermuda shorts.

"Excuse me, gentlemen. Please be reminded that no drinking of alcohol is allowed in public places after 10.30pm at night," one of the pair said politely.

Hades and Hermes looked around their table, slightly confused. Hades spotted the bottle of dessert wine peeking out from his grocery bag.

"Oh that. We weren't drinking. We were just having a chat," he stuffed the bottle deep into the bag emphatically and shifted it from the table to the spot on the bench next to him.

"Right, having a chat," the other police officer said tonelessly. "What's that you have there?"

He pointed at the paper plate on the table, its gooey contents glistening unappealingly.

"Oh, this? It's what we were chatting about," Hermes replied conversationally. "I'm a teacher at an after-school enrichment centre. This week, we will be having a lesson on ritual offerings in ancient Greek history. I was just showing my friend how I plan to conduct the demonstration. This guy's got a PhD in Classics."

Despite himself, Hades snorted.

"And I was telling him what a bad job he's doing," Hades added hastily. "Well, in any case, we were about to clean up and get going."

"You know how the hours slip by when you're catching up with an old friend," Hermes shrugged nonchalantly.

The police officers looked expressionlessly from the two men to the gloopy mess.

"I'm imagining more ... golden ceremonial jars, incense, olive crowns ... that sort of thing?" one of the officers said.

"Yes, and don't they wear those toga thingies and leather sandals, too?" the other added helpfully.

"Ah, yes, well, this is only a rough mock-up. I'll have the works ready for the actual class," Hermes nodded.

"Alright, alright. Good luck with your class," one of the officers replied. "Have a good night, gentlemen."

"And to you, too," Hermes gave a two-fingered salute.

They watched as the officers walked away, off to discover other nocturnal troublemakers.

"Nice guys," Hermes said, watching them go. "You know, Singapore's weather is hot and all, but do you mean to tell me that the police officers here actually wear *that* for their uniform?"

"Nah, those are the community engagement officers. The other lot's still got their spiffy epaulettes, shiny buttons, the works."

"Oh, thank heavens. Zeus forbid that proper uniforms should ever become defunct," Hermes laid a hand on his forehead in mock despair.

"Considering your sartorial choices, perhaps we should institute a uniform ourselves," Hades gave Hermes the once-over again darkly.

"Alright, alright, it's been nice to see you again. How long has it been? Two hundred years? Anyway, you take care of yourself. I'll write you again. Or do you prefer email? Facebook?" Hermes stood up.

"Heavens, no. A letter is fine."

Hermes grinned insufferably once more and threw Hades a two-fingered salute as well.

"See you soon, King of Darkness," he said, turning around a column and promptly disappeared.

9 THE USEFUL FICTION

Sophie was in the midst of trying out a new hibiscus green tea recipe when Mr Chang came into the shop. He was dabbing at his forehead with a handkerchief. It was a hot day outside.

"Hello! I've not seen *you* in a while," Sophie called out.

Mr Chang waved. He folded his handkerchief into a neat square before putting it back into his pocket. Sophie could not help but smile secretly behind her surgical face mask. She hardly knew anyone who still used handkerchiefs these days, let alone have them pressed so impeccably like Mr Chang did. She bet that the handkerchief was embroidered with his initials, too.

"Hi Sophie, how have you been keeping? I'm glad that the flower shop is re-opened to customers now. It must have been hard for you. You had to close for what, two, three months?"

"Yes, we had to close the shop for four months. But it forced me to finally get my e-commerce site up and running," Sophie grinned. "Miraculously, we still received orders online from time to time. With Hades around, I was able to fulfil quite a number of deliveries when the lockdown eased up. In any case, I'm thankful that things seem to be looking up now."

Even with the face mask obscuring half his visage, Sophie could tell that Mr Chang was looking a lot better. The peaky pallor was gone, and his eyes appeared lively and vibrant once more. She was glad.

"How are *you*, Mr Chang? How are things with Miss Lilac Peonies?"

"They're going really well, actually," Mr Chang said, chuckling a little in his usual bashful manner. "The minor … issue we had months earlier was resolved. I'd been meaning to tell you that Hades had been so kind to lend me a listening ear then and had even offered me some advice. I have to say, I think it's because of his suggestions that we really managed to turn things around. I must thank him properly sometime."

"Yes, sure! He's out for a delivery now, but I think he should be back soon. Come, sit down, I need a guinea pig for my new tea recipe."

Mr Chang took his usual seat at the counter and looked around the shop nostalgically. Everything was unchanged. There was the familiar smell of wood and dried flowers that he loved so much. It was cool and dim within, a much-needed respite from the relentless sun beating down on the heated concrete outside. And there was Sophie, her eyes bright and her smile firmly in place. It was always possible to tell when she was smiling, even with her small face half veiled by the surgical mask. Her mere presence was a balm, soothing away all that was fretful and harried. The shop served as a sanctuary for many of her regular customers. It was almost a secret they were reluctant to share with too many others, for fear of spoiling the very tranquillity that they loved so much about Sophie's World.

"Is that a new tea set you have there?" Mr Chang asked.

"Yes," Sophie said somewhat guiltily. "Online shopping has been getting harder and harder to resist!"

She caressed the cool black ceramic of the angular teapot. Its surface was streaked with cracks filled in with golden lacquer in the classic style of Japanese *kintsugi*. It came with four matching teacups. She had ordered it directly from a Japanese craftsman, who had also recently set up an online shop for his age-old trade, passed down from generation to generation dating back to the Meiji era. The exquisite technical execution of the iconic design demonstrated the unmistakeable mastery he had over his craft. The tea set was packaged with great care as well, and had reached Sophie in impeccable condition.

Simply touching it made Sophie feel intimately connected to the immense weight of the ancient, elegant philosophy of *kintsugi*. She loved the idea of bestowing value upon brokenness, imperfection and the transience of all things, revealing flaws to be just as beautiful and worthy of deep contemplation as opulence and extravagance. It was easy to admire the exuberant, the colourful, the flowers in full bloom. But an appreciation for the sparse, the quiet and the lonely aspects of the world was a sensibility that had to be carefully cultivated. Inexplicably, she thought of Hades. At times, he reminded her of a lone bare tree shrouded in mist, nonchalant and peaceful beneath the indifference of an autumnal sky. His loneliness and his strength drew her to him. She longed to be the golden lacquer to fill his cracks.

But it was difficult. As long as they both lived under her mother's roof, there was an unbridgeable distance between them. Sophie thought then of how well her mother had weathered the pandemic and sighed a little with relief. She had recovered well from her broken hip and had even seemed to have taken a turn for the better in mental acuity. There were many more days when she recognised Sophie, addressed her directly and reminisced about her childhood. At times, Sophie felt she could almost forget her mother's dementia. They indulged in diving deep into pockets of the past, as vividly as if they were reliving it. The months she spent in lockdown at home with her mother made Sophie feel like a child again, squirrelled away safely in the little fortress of their apartment. She started reading books again. Afternoons flew by in a cosy blur as she lost herself in fictional worlds. She read and she napped, and she worked on the occasional online or phone orders for floral deliveries. Hades bought their meals and groceries, and delivered the finished bouquets to the customers.

So, despite the pandemic having cruelly taken the lives and livelihoods of countless others in the world, Sophie felt coddled and insulated from the reality of the disaster, doted on as she was by both Hades and her mother. The pandemic affected different people so differently. The scale of devastation was tilted so unevenly, Sophie almost felt a sense of guilt for not having suffered as much as many of her compatriots did.

"How unfair life is," she said wonderingly at that thought.

"Hmm?" Mr Chang was blowing at the surface of his teacup.

"Hey, don't do that! Just be patient and wait for it to cool down on its own," Sophie scolded him, her hands planted on her hips in mock anger.

"Okay," he replied, obediently setting the cup back down on the counter.

They watched the steam rise from the cups.

"Actually, I'm here to place an order for a bouquet," Mr Chang said abruptly. "It's a special one."

Sophie leaned forward eagerly. "Well?"

"I … er … I want to propose to Amanda," Mr Chang said bashfully. "That's her name, by the way, Miss Lilac Peonies."

"Amanda," Sophie savoured the name as though it was that of an exotic species of flower. "How lovely, Mr Chang. This is such great news. I'm so, so happy!"

She smiled so broadly it was infectious. Mr Chang started grinning too, albeit timidly.

"You know me, Sophie. I'm bad at this sort of things. I really need your help."

"There is nothing to it, but to ask a sincere question and to await her truthful answer," Sophie shrugged. "I'm sure that you should know her well enough by now, and how she would want to be asked. Even if you aren't sure, there's really nothing to worry about. Just pick a time and place to tell her what's on your mind, and what you want of her."

She smiled. "But, of course, armed with the most beautiful bouquet made to order by Sophie's World!"

Mr Chang nodded vigorously. "Yes, of course. That's why I'm here. There's no way I could do this without your help."

"Flowers are merely beautiful things to accentuate your sincerity. They are by no means the focal point of a marriage proposal. Neither is the engagement ring, by the way … Oh, have you bought it yet?"

Mr Chang did not miss the slightly contradictory sentiments and laughed.

"Yes, I did," he said, rooting around his briefcase. "Here it is."

Sophie's eyes widened as the diamond sparkled into sight. It was simply enormous.

"My word! Mr Chang," Sophie gasped. "Just how many months' worth of salary is this? Wait, never mind, don't tell me. I don't really want to know."

Mr Chang was pleased with her reaction. He had spent hours at the jeweller's, picking out the pear-shaped diamond. It was encircled with smaller diamonds, making it look even bigger than it already was. The delicate, narrow band was also encrusted with tiny diamonds, ensuring that the ring caught the light from all possible angles. It was a stunning ring, fit for a princess.

"Amanda, oh, Amanda. What a treat he has in store for you," Sophie said in a sing-song voice, happily turning the ring around to admire it from all angles. She held it by its box, the ring still nestled securely in its cushioned seat. There was no way she would lay a finger on the ring itself for fear of leaving the tiniest bit of fingerprint smudge. She had to preserve its pristine splendour at all cost.

"This magnificent ring is simply crying out for an equally magnificent bouquet to complement it," Sophie declared, setting the box down on the counter gingerly. "Leave it to me, Mr Chang. I will create the perfect bouquet, resplendent enough to match the grandeur of the ring, while at the same time simple enough to serve only as its frame, to accentuate the ring's beauty, but not overshadowing it."

She was breathless from talking so quickly. Ideas and images churned furiously in her mind's eye. She could not wait to get to work.

"Oh, but Sophie, I've not set a date and time yet. I've not

planned … anything! Hang on, let's not get too ahead of ourselves yet."

"What? Ahead of ourselves?" Sophie exclaimed, aggrieved. "Mr Chang! How could you walk in here with such an exciting client brief and expect me to restrain myself? Mr Chang, you have to set the date and time for your proposal *right now*."

Mr Chang cowered beneath her withering glare. "Now …? I mean … I don't know … There's still a pandemic going on, you know? I don't want to …"

"Stop right there. Pandemic or no pandemic, I can see that you've made up your mind to marry this woman. You've bought this ginormous ring. You've walked into my shop. I know you've rehearsed in your mind what you are going to say. *You are ready*, Mr Chang," Sophie cried, seizing him by his wrists and shaking them with conviction.

"Argh! Sophie!" Mr Chang laughed and struggled. "Stop that! Alright, alright! You're right, I am ready. I guess I was just … afraid. I needed you to push me in the right direction."

"And push I shall. Call her now, ask her to meet you tonight."

"To … tonight? I mean, I'm ready, but I'm not sure if I'm *that* ready …"

Sophie glared at him, waving the ring box about in a slightly threatening manner.

"Are you hemming and hawing right now? Are you sure you want to marry Amanda? It seems like you're not so sure after all," she said ambivalently, closing the lid of the box emphatically, shutting down the sparkle of the diamond. "Come back again when you're ready, okay?"

"No! No, that's not true. I *am* sure. I've never been so sure of anything in my entire life," Mr Chang cut in. "Alright. I'm going to call her now. Wait for me, okay?"

Sophie hid her giggle behind her face mask and watched as Mr Chang walked out the door with his phone in hand. She could see his other hand creeping in his pocket, seeking the comfort of his handkerchief.

"Was I too much of a bully?" she wondered aloud.

"You're *always* a bully," a male voice responded suddenly behind her, making her jump.

"What! When did you arrive?" Sophie shrieked.

"Oh, I came in through the back door. It was a shorter route, from where I was returning," Hades replied casually, reaching for his apron on the wall. "Why are you so startled? Guilty conscience?"

"Maybe," Sophie said, smiling. "I've just bullied Mr Chang into arranging his marriage proposal date."

"I overheard the tail end of your conversation."

"Yeah, well. Mr Chang and I have been friends for quite some time. I know that he came here for that push he needed. From the pushy person that is me!"

"That you are," Hades said fondly.

Suddenly, he grew serious. "Sophie, there's something I need to tell you. I have been summoned by my brother, Zeus. I'm meeting him tonight, at his holiday home in Sentosa Cove."

"Your brother … Zeus. Zeus, the leader of all the Olympian gods?"

"Yes."

"Oh," Sophie said, feeling small. She knew it could not be

good news. Perhaps Hades had to return to the Underworld soon after all.

"I'll tell you more later," Hades said, as Mr Chang came back into the shop, mopping his brow again.

"She said she can't make it tonight. But she will be free tomorrow evening. I've made a reservation at the restaurant where we had our first date," Mr Chang was breathless with elation.

"Tomorrow evening! Right-o! I'll work on the bouquet tomorrow, then, so it will be fresh and ready for you to collect just before you go," Sophie beamed.

"Sounds good," Mr Chang climbed back onto his stool. "Oh hey, Hades! You're back."

"Hey, good to see you, Chang. You look well," Hades replied.

"Yes, I've been meaning to thank you for the advice you gave me. I've had no ... er ... further problems since then," Mr Chang told him gratefully. "Let's go out for a round of drinks sometime, on me."

"Without me?" Sophie pouted.

"Oh, of course not, let's all go together!" Mr Chang added.

"Yes, if your marriage proposal goes well, we can celebrate," Sophie smiled. "I can't wait! I'm so happy, just imagining the future Mr and Mrs Chang."

"Er," Mr Chang coughed. "Sophie, I've never had the chance to correct you all this while, but 'Chang' is not my surname. My full name is Ng Quan Chang. All my friends call me Chang. So, er, technically ... when I first introduced myself to you ... your addition of the salutation was ... unnecessary."

"What? You've never corrected me all this while?" Sophie wailed in embarrassment. "How could you, Mr Chang? Argh! And now I've already gotten too used to it!"

"It's alright," Mr Chang made a vague waving motion, laughing. "I'm used to it now, too."

"Oh, wait, may I show Hades the ring?" Sophie's eyes sparkled.

Mr Chang nodded. Sophie cracked the small box open and flashed the diamond ring in Hades' face.

"Nice, right?"

"Yes, it's … er … very shiny," Hades nodded.

"You mean to say you don't know your carats from your carrots?" Sophie teased.

"Er … no … I don't," Hades admitted, hanging his head.

"Well, actually, neither do I," Sophie poked him playfully. "All I can tell is that Mr Chang had put a lot of heart into picking this one out, and I'm sure Amanda will be very happy with it."

"You think so?" Mr Chang said, a note of doubt creeping into his voice. "I tried my best to pick what I thought she would like. I do hope she likes it."

"She will," Sophie reassured him. "It's a gift from you! That's all that matters. And just look at you! Do you remember that day when we were debating if *yuanfen* exists? *Yuanfen*, that is, the magic of the improbable; the seemingly supernatural force behind one thing happening instead of another. How do you feel now? Do you think she is fated to be with you?"

"Well, I admit I've not given it much thought," Mr Chang said. "It would be nice to believe that destiny exists, and that we are fated to be together. Because if that's the case, then

I don't ever have to wonder if there's actually someone out there who is … better suited for me. And when the going gets tough, we would be more inclined to work things out rather than to give up and simply find someone else."

"Did you ever wonder about that whilst you were dating? If there might be someone better out there? Did you still continue to check the dating app after meeting Amanda?" Sophie mused.

"That's the thing. Among the many ladies I've met through the dating app, Amanda was the one I liked immediately because she didn't give off the vibe that she was assessing me as a potential candidate to be accepted or rejected. She didn't approach our first meeting with that kind of a mindset. Or, at least, I don't think she did."

"What was it like then?"

"Well, I felt like I was … making a new friend. She was open and sincere and … curious about me. And that made me feel like finding out more about her, too. And gradually, we did become friends before we became lovers. I don't know if Amanda ever checked the dating app again after meeting me, but she didn't make me feel like she did, or that I was being measured against comparable options from which she could easily pick and choose. She made me feel a genuine human connection. And that is why she is special. It became easy for me not to feel like checking the dating app anymore. I was simply enjoying her company so much."

Sophie nodded along, her eyes wide. "This is fascinating. I'm so glad that you *can* find true love on a dating app after all. I feel like what you've said has taught me something about the concept of *yuanfen*. Perhaps it's a useful fiction, which is nice to have, but, contrary to what I had believed, not something that we really need after all."

"What do you mean when you say 'useful fiction'?" Mr Chang asked.

"Well, the existence of *yuanfen* or – its closely related cousin – destiny, cannot be proved or disproved using scientific methodology, as far as we know. Science has yet to come to a conclusion if all of past, present and future, as we experience it, is merely an illusion, a construct of our brains as it were, and that everything that will happen has already happened. If time is an illusion, we might be merely walking down a path that has already been paved, and there's nothing we can do to change it."

"In that case, we don't have any free will," Hades added.

"We *feel* like we do, but if destiny exists, then that feeling is also merely an illusion," Sophie expounded.

"An illusion that we are actually making choices in our lives?"

"Yes," Sophie said emphatically. "You *think* you are making a choice, but in reality, you have essentially *already* made that choice, because it was fated to be, so there's no way you could have acted otherwise."

"But why does it feel so *real*? It feels so real that I just chose having laksa over chicken rice for lunch just now," Hades laughed. "So, there's no possible world in which I could have chosen chicken rice? What about in a parallel universe? What if, whenever we are confronted with choices, both choices *are* made? At that point in time, the universe splits into two parallel universes – one in which I had laksa, and the other in which I had chicken rice."

"In this case, you are saying that destiny does not exist. Rather, every single choice a person could possibly encounter in life *does happen*, all at the same time, in different parallel universes. There would then have to be an infinite number of parallel universes, what with all the minutest choices we have to make!" Sophie pondered. "That's an interesting theory, but we can't prove it scientifically, either. It would be just as viable a story as the idea of *yuanfen*."

"So, is that why you used the term useful 'fiction'? Because we have different competing narratives of the world, all of which cannot be scientifically proven or disproven, and we should then just pick the one that is most useful to us? But, useful for what, exactly?" Hades challenged.

"I don't know, happiness maybe? A sense of contentment and fulfilment? An end to the choice overload effect? As opposed to having our Mr Chang here spiralling endlessly into an infinite catalogue of potential mates and becoming paralysed into not making a decision at all, he could act *as if* destiny exists, that he was fated to meet Amanda, to fall in love with her and to live happily ever after with her," Sophie answered.

"Knowing that it might not be true?"

"Yes, I suppose so. If it helps to make life easier. And to make their marriage stronger. If they both believe that they are meant to be together, then they will move mountains to stay together, no matter how difficult life gets."

Mr Chang raised a hand nervously. He had been darting his gaze back and forth from Sophie to Hades like a spectator at a tennis match.

"I think I'm lost. I'm not quite following the discussion."

Sophie turned to him and smiled apologetically. "I'm sorry, sometimes I get ahead of myself. I forget that not everybody likes discussing lofty, abstract ideas like I do."

"As the ordinary non-philosophical layman, what if I were to abandon the concept of destiny altogether? Just … you know … go with the flow. I'm proposing to Amanda because I want to. If she says yes, we will get married because we want to. It doesn't matter if we are in fact destined to be together. It's good enough that in this life, we met, we made the choice to be together, and that's that," Mr Chang ventured.

"Of course, that's the default position everybody takes. When you're happy, you don't need philosophy. It is my sincerest hope that you both never have to encounter the hard questions. I'm not trying to be a wet blanket. I'm just thinking about it, from a detached, objective point of view. A general point of view, if you will, of *all* human relationships. You are a good man, Mr Chang, and you are not greedy. But I know plenty of men who will agonise over whether a particular lady is the 'best possible catch' for them, even if they get along just fine. That is when it gets tricky, don't you think?"

"Yes, I think I see what you mean, Sophie," Mr Chang said. "No relationship is perfectly smooth-sailing, and the rocky patches are precisely when you start to question if the both of you are truly meant to be together."

"Yes, you get it now!" Sophie cried. "To stay together, or to find someone else? That is the question everyone secretly asks in their hearts when … *that* quarrel gets really unpleasant, *that* disagreement seemingly intractable. That would be the kind of situation in which you would have to decide if you believe in fate or not."

"What about the simple method of weighing pros and cons? If a couple were considering a divorce, they could just list out the pros and cons of staying together and separating from one another … I don't know, use a Pugh Matrix calculation?" Mr Chang considered.

"Maybe that's what people do," Sophie said evenly. "Though I shudder at the thought of making such a list! A romantic relationship is not a business partnership. Somehow, I think it would be much more difficult to make a decision based on economic or pragmatic reasons."

"That's true," Mr Chang conceded.

"Sophie, the man's gearing up for his marriage proposal! What's all this talk about divorce and separation? Come on, get it together," Hades commanded.

"Yes, what's wrong with me?" Sophie shrieked. "It's a happy day today. I'm so glad that you came to me with this piece of good news, Mr Chang. Forget all that philosophical nonsense, and just focus on what you are going to say to Amanda. Everything will be just fine."

"I'm going to tell her that we are meant to be together," Mr Chang announced. "Everything that had ever happened in my life thus far has led to me asking her to be my wife. If anything had been different, no matter how seemingly insignificant, it may have entirely changed the course of my life and I would not have met her. When I think about it this way, how can I not say that *yuanfen* exists?"

Sophie smiled mistily. "I'm so glad that you finally found the woman whom you can feel this way about. The feeling that … even if you had a time machine, you would not use it to go back in time to correct any regrets or misgivings, because of the risk that any changes, no matter how small, could lead to a ripple effect resulting in you not meeting her at all. Don't you agree?"

"Yes, that is exactly how I feel," Mr Chang affirmed. "Alright, I'm going home now to rehearse my speech for tomorrow. I'll leave the ring in your good care, okay?"

"I'll weave it into the bouquet beautifully. Leave it to me," Sophie said, making a shooing motion with her hands.

"No, wait, I have to pay for the tea," Mr Chang reminded her.

As the pair of friends huddled over the cash register, Hades wondered to himself what Sophie would do if *she* had a time machine.

They waved as Mr Chang left the shop with a noticeable spring in his step. Sophie turned to Hades.

"I haven't forgotten. Why did Zeus summon you?" she asked, concern in her eyes.

"It's the pandemic. It has caused an uncharacteristically large influx of souls into the Underworld and overwhelmed our processing capacities. There is a huge backlog of unjudged souls and some of them have leaked into Poseidon's domain, causing him a great deal of inconvenience. I suspect that I would have to do some damage control, and ... return to the Underworld to set things in order."

So, the time had come then. Sophie shifted her gaze downward. She busied herself with washing up the used tea set and carefully setting its components out to dry. There was so much she wanted to ask Hades. *Will you be coming back? When?*

Hades took the last teacup from her hands and set it on the drying rack himself.

"Sophie," he said solemnly. "Will you close the shop early today and go on a date with me?"

"What, now?" she exclaimed, startled. She looked down at her dirty work apron.

"Yes, now," Hades said. "Come with me?"

Sophie hesitated, casting a glance at the clock on the wall. *Oh, what the hell.*

"Alright then, let's go on our first date," she said, smiling up at Hades. For a moment, her heart constricted at those kind eyes of his that she had grown so familiar with. "Where do you want to go?"

"I've always wanted to try riding a tandem bicycle with you," Hades said casually.

"What?"

"Can't you ride a bicycle?"

"Yes, I can, but of all things, why riding a bicycle?"

"I don't know," Hades shrugged. "It's such a human thing to do. So, do you want to go with me?"

"Alright, alright, let's go."

~*~

Sophie was screaming.

"Wait! You're going too fast!" she panted, trying to match Hades' speed on her pedals. They kept swooshing out from under her feet. She scrambled to re-insert her feet into her pedals as they flew round and round in maddening circles.

"What? This is too fast?" Hades turned around, puzzled.

"Yes!"

"Well, then, we might as well walk if we're going to be so slow."

Sophie swatted Hades on his back, annoyed. "Haven't you heard of a leisurely bike ride? Just to feel the wind in your hair and the sun on your face? Nice and easy, enjoying the trees and the greenery and the ocean around us?"

"Alright, you sit in the front then," Hades suggested, swinging himself off the seat and offering it to Sophie. "Let's switch places!"

"Does it make a difference?"

"We won't know till we try, right?"

"Okay," Sophie said, hopping off the back of the tandem bicycle.

They switched places and now Sophie set the pace.

"Argh! It's so much more difficult being the one in front! You're so heavy!" she complained, straining every muscle in her legs to pedal.

"I'm pedalling, I'm pedalling!" Hades shouted to her helpfully.

"Okay! I'm doing my best!" Sophie yelled back. Sweat was pouring down her temples. "This feels totally different from riding a normal bicycle!"

Hades laughed, a booming sound that recalled distant thunder.

"You're so slow! I feel like I'm making no difference whether I pedal or not!" he called out to her.

Sophie grunted, dashing the sweat from her eyes. She was determined with every cell in her body to succeed.

~*~

After an agonising fifteen minutes, Sophie gave up. She felt as though her calves would break off entirely from under her knees.

"Let's rest for a while," she said, stopping the bicycle. She was utterly winded.

Hades tossed her a bottle of water. "You rest. Come, hop on, I'll take us on the scenic, leisurely bike ride you wanted."

He helped her onto the rear seat once more. "You be the rear admiral. I'll be the captain."

"Rear admiral? I'll admire your rear alright," Sophie winked.

"You're terrible," he informed her. "Hold tight and keep your feet off the pedals and on the frame, okay?"

"Okay."

Hades took up the steersman seat once again and made a show of stretching out his muscles.

"Are you ready?" he called out to Sophie.

"Yes, Sir!" she yelled in response.

And off they went. The bicycle whizzed along the wide paths of the public park like greased lightning. The trees shot past her in a blur. Sophie could see the ocean, peeking out from between the tree trunks, sparkling and dancing beneath the sun. Despite herself, she laughed with joy. She could not remember the last time she had sat on a bicycle. Birdsong emerged as they entered a slightly more wooded area. She saw a pair of butterflies chasing each other, tracing a trail of happiness in the air.

Hades slowed down as the path narrowed. He steered them into the shade and kept up a genuinely leisurely pace this time. His shoulders were broad and sturdy. Sophie thought that they could take on the weight of the world. She started to feel a little pensive as the surroundings grew quieter. Her thoughts seemed too loud in her head.

They gradually sped out of the little shaded woodland and headed to the beach. Hades parked the bicycle against a large raintree that overlooked a small rocky corner. They sat down on the rocks, removed their shoes and plunged their feet into the sea. He had bought her an ice cream from a nearby kiosk.

"Hades, this is so nice," Sophie said, smiling up at him.

"It was nice when you finally stopped screaming on that damned bicycle," he replied.

"You were going too fast! It was so dangerous!" she shot back.

"You're always safe with me, Sophie," Hades said, lowering his head and nipped her on the nose with his fingers.

Sophie caught his fingers, smiling. She did not let go. With both her hands, she opened his large palm and slipped her right hand into it, closing it tightly. He brought their clasped hands to his lap. They let out a sigh at the exact same time, looked at each other in shock and burst into laughter.

It soon subsided and they lapsed into silence.

"Thank you, Sophie, for the date. It was a lot of fun," Hades said finally.

"Is this ... your way of saying goodbye to me?" Sophie whispered. She could feel the familiar, threatening sting rising in her eyes and willed herself fiercely not to cry.

"I don't know," Hades replied honestly. "I just didn't want to return to the Underworld without having asked you out properly."

Sophie swallowed hard. She could feel her vision swimming. She blinked repeatedly, concentrating on the warmth that enveloped her hand. She squeezed his hand very hard.

"Erm … Ow … That hurts," Hades said as politely as he could.

"Oh, sorry," Sophie let go abruptly, but he caught her hand again and cradled it gently in both his hands like a small animal.

Sophie let her head fall against his shoulder. They both looked at the ocean.

"The sun is going down," she murmured.

"Yes," he answered.

10 ZEUS' DECREE

"What's the point of being a god if you're still going to get hangovers?" Zeus complained, as Hades walked into his swanky beachfront vacation home at Sentosa Cove.

Hades curled the edge of a lip in disgust. "Brother, you look like a caricature."

Zeus was lounging on an expensive-looking black leather sofa, clad in a white hotel bathrobe and its matching flimsy bedroom slippers. The robe gaped obscenely at his abdomen, its hem flapping about loosely around the knees. He had draped a heavy gold chain around his well-sculpted neck. A cigar in one hand and a glass of whiskey in another, Zeus shrugged.

"There's always some modicum of truth in stereotypes, isn't there?"

He had taken on an extremely handsome mortal form, albeit with an unsettling bit of Ted Bundy about the eyes. He did not look true to the stereotype; that would typically have been an unattractive balding, middle-aged man with a jutting beer gut. Zeus gave himself generous six-pack abs and thick wavy hair. He could not resist, however, a closely cropped salt-and-pepper beard that at least grounded his overall look with some dignity and gravitas.

"If you're going to sport such a pretty boy look, why not wear something nice at least? I can see your ball sack in that," Hades said in a most disgruntled manner.

Zeus roared with laughter and carelessly adjusted the flaps of his robe so they properly covered his privates. He grinned leeringly at Hades.

"You haven't changed one bit, brother. I guess I just have a thing for hotel bathrobes, you know! They make me feel like one of those mortal playboy billionaires. Come, sit down! Have a drink. Don't be so stiff!"

Hades leaned against a wall. "No thanks, I'd rather stand. You haven't changed either." He looked round the swanky house. It was so predictably luxurious. "Something seems to be missing from this scene though."

"Oh, I've sent the nymphs away," Zeus waved a hand about dismissively. "This is serious business we're discussing, eh? Now where's that Demeter! Hermes is getting tardy!"

"No, I'm just early," Hades said indifferently.

"Brother, brother, this whole matter is most unlike you," Zeus squinted at Hades keenly. "You've always been the responsible one, the reliable one! Unlike the rest of us degenerate lot. I was most surprised to hear that you let the ball drop on this one."

There was a cold glint in Hades' eyes. "Have I, now?"

"Your loyal minions are too scared to admit that they can't handle the problem without you! Those vain three care too much about what their boss thinks of them," Zeus scoffed, pausing to refill his whiskey glass.

"Minos, Aeacus and Rhadamanthus have never let me down," Hades admitted. "This disaster must be something of an unprecedented scale. Well, I won't deny it. I should have been more discerning."

"Nah, it's perfectly fine to go on a holiday every few centuries or so," Zeus waved his cigar in the air. "You deserve it! You work the hardest among us! It's just that Poseidon has been complaining my ear off about those poor waiting souls who leaked out of the Underworld and started possessing his sea creatures. You can imagine the pandemonium on the affected coasts! It's complete chaos. As Ruler of the Dead, you've just gotta help clean that mess up."

"Yes, I know, I'm planning to," Hades sighed, folding his arms. "Is Poseidon angry enough at me to want to fight me? You know how much time he wastes on such unnecessary things."

"I don't know, brother. It sure doesn't look good," Zeus downed his freshly poured whiskey in a single gulp. "You two sort it out. Just try not to … break anything, yeah?"

"You really just mean your temple in Athens, right?" Hades scoffed. "Right, I'll be sure to keep that in mind as Poseidon flings small mountains and lightning bolts at me."

"Alright, alright, I'll speak to him first," Zeus said flippantly. "We're all brothers, yeah? This is just a small hiccup. Nothing to fuss over."

"Yes, you tell that to Poseidon," Hades replied darkly.

Just then, Hermes breezed into the house with Demeter trailing sullenly behind him.

"Demeter, my dear, it's been a long time," Zeus stood up, attempting to kiss her on the cheek.

Demeter dodged his advances and sat down heavily on one of the elegant armchairs.

"Abuse of authority? Seriously?" she glared at him. "This is no simple accusation to make. I hope you have evidence to back that claim."

Zeus sighed and touched the whiskey glass to his forehead.

"Come on, Demeter, Hades, we're all immortals here. Let's not make things difficult for each other," he spread his arms apathetically, looking from one surly face to another.

Hades refused to look at Demeter. He remained resolutely on his feet, half in shadow as he crossed his arms impatiently.

"I have to say, *some* immortals don't seem to understand the idea that our powers come with responsibilities," he said off-handedly. "*Some* immortals even employ the most devious methods of deception and emotional manipulation, just to keep their children by their side."

"*Some* immortals should stay put where they belong and stop meddling around in the mortal realm where they don't belong," Demeter shot back. "*Some* immortals speak loftily of responsibilities but yet neglect their very own without a care in the world."

Zeus looked at both of them and sighed. He gestured for Hermes to join him on the sofa and poured him a stiff drink.

"This new infectious disease pandemic … it's a mess. How did it start? Did you really do it?" Zeus addressed Demeter directly.

Though she was in the form of a mortal old lady, Demeter showed not an ounce of frailty or vulnerability at that moment.

"You can't prove if it was or wasn't me. Let's see, what are the odds? Option one, a chance genetic mutation in *one* out of the tens of thousands of different strains of zoonotic viruses, leading to transmissibility from animal to human. Or option two, the agentic act of a goddess, seeking to sow discord and suffering among humans for no good reason at all. I know which option most people would bet their money on."

"Stop giving us that false dilemma crap. There *was* motive for you to have done it. You did it to come between Persephone and I," Hades said, locking eyes with her now, not bothering to conceal the intense fury that burned in him.

"There is no *Persephone and you*. Persephone is my daughter. She belongs to me, by my side," Demeter answered.

"Have you ever asked her if that is what she wants? You keep her by your side using underhanded means, by lying to her for years! Pretending to be ill! I've got to give it to you though, getting your hip broken just to punish her for coming to the Underworld with me was really something."

"It's just a mortal shell," Demeter said indifferently. "Yes, it was painful, but I'm sure you know now that physical pain is nothing but a small nuisance to us."

"But the emotional pain and distress you caused Persephone is certainly no *small nuisance* to her at all! Damn you, have you even for one second in your entire life considered the feelings of your daughter? Have you thought about how it feels like to have to dedicate your life to caring for an aged, frail mother, facing a rollercoaster of emotions from the very painful experience of witnessing the effects of dementia? This is no joking matter! And yet, you *used* it, so cruelly, to serve your own interests!"

Hades felt as though a dam had broken within him. All the pent-up rage that he carried inside him all those months whilst living with Sophie roared into life with all the force of a tropical squall.

Demeter stared at Hades coldly. "Just how long have you known Persephone, Hades? Do you think you know her better than her own mother? Persephone is a caregiver by nature. She needs to express this in her life for it to be meaningful and fulfilling. I know her emotional needs much better than you think you do. Just what do you plan to offer her, hmm? A throne by your side down in the Underworld? Do you think she will be happy, to take on the duties and responsibilities of Queen of the Underworld?"

At that, Hades was stunned into silence. He was, indeed, not sure at all. Demeter had a point about Sophie's personality. He had, even in the short time they spent together, sensed the nature of the fundamental driving force within Sophie. It was her essence, if there was such a thing, to help and to soothe and to calm. There were times when he felt that she lived for such interactions, that her flower shop was only a conduit for her to engage in activities of this nature. She was happiest when she was able to help another.

"The way she lived before you arrived was the best possible life for her. She was easily spurred to feelings of happiness on a regular basis, simply when I recognised her as my daughter. She felt meaning in her day-to-day work at the flower shop. She was able to create what essentially is her art, through the medium of floral arrangement. She would lose herself for hours on end, engrossed in the process, losing all track of time. She had many close friends and got along well with all her customers. Her shop was a business she started herself, her *own world*, as the very name suggests. And now, you come along and make her fall in love with you … and then what? You can't stay in the mortal realm with her. You belong in the Underworld."

Demeter stopped, slightly out of breath. Sighing, she poured herself a drink from Zeus' extensive collection.

"It doesn't matter whether or not I caused the pandemic. As things stand now, you are needed back in the Underworld, where you belong. You should return and never come back again. Persephone had a happy life before she met you. She will continue to lead a happy life even after you're gone."

There was a sharp intake of breath by Hades. "So, you're saying that meeting me has changed absolutely nothing? That she could blithely forget all about my existence, and go on as she had before?"

"That's exactly what I'm saying," Demeter said, her eyes piercing. "If you love her, *truly* love her, this should be what you would want for her as well."

"Just hang on a minute," Zeus boomed, his speech slightly slurring after the many glasses of whiskey he had downed throughout their conversation. "Do you mean to say my little brother is *in love?*"

He pushed himself off of the sofa and staggered unsteadily to Hades, still holding the whiskey glass. "Brother! Hades! You *love* this woman, Persephone?"

Zeus clasped him by his shoulders, shaking him eagerly like a crazed man. The small amount of whiskey left in the glass sloshed around precariously. Hades remained silent, letting Zeus do whatever he wanted. Zeus had started laughing uproariously, hanging his head and allowing it to collide haphazardly against Hades' chest. He was swaying comically like a drunken sailor in an old film.

"My brother, my brother, my solemn and boring old brother, Hades! In love!" Zeus shouted happily. He let go of Hades and danced around nattily, flinging splashes of whiskey everywhere.

Demeter, Hermes and Hades waited patiently as Zeus galloped and pranced all around the living room, just about narrowly missing a tumble into the decorative koi pond built right in the middle of the house.

"Hades and Persephone, sitting in a tree, K-I-S-S-I-N-G!" he chanted, twirling himself round and round.

"Er, *that*, Sir, has gone rather out of fashion amongst the children these days," Hermes added helpfully. "It's very last century."

Wiping tears of mirth from his eyes, Zeus staggered back to the small gathering and flung himself gracelessly onto the sofa. His bathrobe flapped open obscenely once more. Nobody bothered to say a thing.

"My, oh my. Hades, are you saying that you wish to take Persephone as your bride? To rule as the Queen of the Underworld with you?" Zeus said, finally more sober.

Hades said nothing. *Did he have the right to wish that?*

"That's what he wants, of course," Demeter intoned. "You might as well admit it now, Hades. Let's settle the matter once and for all. This is what we are all here for."

"It's not just my wish that matters. It's what Sophie wants that matters too," Hades broke his silence.

"Sophie wouldn't know what is best for her. She wouldn't even know what would make her happy. But I am her mother, and I know. She will not be happy in that dark accursed Underworld of yours. She belongs here, among the light and the living and the joyful."

"We can't presume to know everything about a whole other person without giving her the chance to speak for herself," Hades replied testily.

"Come now, Demeter," Zeus said cajolingly. "Hades is the best guy there is! Don't you want Persephone to experience the joys of marriage? As Queen of the Underworld, she would have the authority to shape her role and responsibilities to best suit her strengths and inclinations. There are grievances and misery aplenty in the Underworld that would benefit from her sweet, helping nature."

"The Underworld is the realm of the *dead*. Which mother would want her daughter to spend her days aimlessly concerning herself with the sordid matters of the souls of the dead? And about the joys of marriage, I can't say I have had the experience myself," Demeter said pointedly at Zeus.

Hasty to change the subject, Zeus slapped the armrest of the sofa. "It seems like we have reached a stalemate! Of course, eventually, I have to make a decision, whether or not either of you would be happy about it. But right now, I don't have sufficient information. I want to hear from Persephone herself. Hermes, go fetch Persephone, please."

"Certainly, Sir," Hermes gave an exaggerated bow.

"Leave the matter of the pandemic and the mortals out of this. They are not relevant to the issue at hand," Demeter said.

"Is that so? That sounds to me like an admission of guilt. Demeter, if you had a hand in causing the pandemic, you ought to be ashamed of yourself. It has gone way out of hand. Knowing you, perhaps you hadn't intended it to. But well over a million mortal lives in just under a year is completely unacceptable," Zeus said, suddenly severe.

Demeter did not say anything. She sat there quietly, just as she did every evening, as Hanna or Sophie spooned porridge into her mouth. Hades could feel his chest ache with his fury restrained. As if of their own accord, his fists clenched and unclenched themselves spasmodically.

Thanks to Hermes' winged sandals, he returned just as swiftly as he had left, with Sophie in hand.

~*~

Sophie blinked and looked around the opulent house Hermes had brought her to. As with every other Singaporean, she had heard of the Sentosa Cove luxury houses but had never actually been in one herself. It was vast and sprawling, with precious antiques and beautiful paintings accentuating every nook and every wall. There was a huge glass window, extending from floor to ceiling, its shutters unfurled to show off the view of the sea. The surface of the water reflected an almost perfect image of the crescent moon high in the sky. The rug beneath her feet was softer than anything she had ever touched. She hoped it was not of animal origin.

"Have a seat, Persephone, once you're done gawking at my house," Zeus grinned, pleased to see that she was clearly impressed by her surroundings.

"I'm sorry," Sophie turned to face the small gathering. She started in confusion when her gaze alighted on her mother, seated calmly at a large leather armchair with gilded claws for feet. "Mother? Is she … Is she alright? Why have you brought her here?"

She addressed Zeus directly, trying to ignore his odd choice of outfit. Her gaze was steady and intrepid. It flickered only momentarily when she met Hades' eyes. He could see that she was determined to present a courageous front.

"Welcome, Persephone," Zeus boomed, ignoring her question. "I am Zeus. Thank you for gracing us with your presence. We are gathered here today to make an important decision. About your future, in fact."

Sophie glanced at Hades. He was standing against the wall impassively, a scowl firmly affixed on his face. Her mother was sitting quietly, serenely, not saying a word.

"Zeus, I'm ... pleased to meet you, Sir," Sophie said, remembering her manners. "How may I be of assistance?"

"It's really quite simple," Zeus began. "I require my brother here, Hades, God of the Underworld, to resume his duties immediately and to remain in the Underworld for the foreseeable future."

Sophie looked at Hades. She sought out his eyes, questioningly. She wished she could touch him, to be near to him. At the moment, he seemed as remote as a stranger. She felt a little afraid.

"Your mother, Persephone, is Goddess of the Harvest," Zeus continued. "She is, of course, currently in her mortal form, and I understand that she lives out the full lifespan of each one she takes on. It's in the nature of her duties as Goddess of the Harvest to be close to the living, to serve *on the ground*, as it were. The pantheon of the gods require deities such as herself to ensure that we do not lose touch with the mortal realm. We need to stay current and relevant. Demeter has lived many mortal lifetimes now, and for each, you were and will always be her daughter. That is the way of the world. This is the way we had been storied into being."

Sophie blinked feverishly at the sudden influx of information. Her brain felt numb and overloaded. "Erm. Do you mind if I sit down?"

"Of course! How rude of me! Come, have a seat!" Zeus smacked a giant palm to his forehead. "Let me get you a drink. What's your poison? Wine? Sherry?"

"Erm … Can I just have a glass of water, please?" Sophie replied.

Hermes grinned. "I'll get it," he said, disappearing into the kitchen.

Sophie sat down at a random chair nearest to her. From her vantage point, she could see both her mother and Hades. Zeus loomed large in her field of vision, showy and vivid with his restless pacing and expansive gesticulations. She saw that her mother sat so quietly, not saying anything. Sophie wondered if she was scared, or if she knew what was going on. But she seemed calm and unperturbed at the moment, so Sophie was not too worried yet. At least Sophie was there to comfort her should anything happen. The new factoid about her mother being the Goddess of the Harvest swam about uncomfortably in her head, as if trying to find the right niche to be slotted into. So, she had met the actual God of the Underworld, and the King of the Olympian Gods, and now … her mother was a goddess too? Sophie felt a little light-headed. It was all still not sinking in properly.

If Mummy is a goddess, then … why was she stricken with dementia? Did gods and goddesses get sick too? Sophie did not know much about the ancient Greek pantheon. She did not think she even learned it in school. Fretful and unsettled, she sat on her hands to stop herself from nibbling at her nails. The questions burned in her chest but she did not know if it was appropriate to ask.

Hermes had returned with a glass of water. Sophie accepted it gratefully and took a giant sip. The coolness calmed her a little and she felt better. She set the glass down on the coffee table carefully and peered around curiously.

Zeus was filling his whiskey glass judiciously. Bottles with different labels were strewn haphazardly across the table, some already empty. Sophie wanted to offer her mother her glass of water, but before she could move, Zeus spoke again. His voice commanded the room. It was the sort of voice that seemed to bodily push all thoughts from its recipients' minds, swarming them, conquering them. Sophie sat up straight, her hands folded neatly on her lap.

"My brother, Hades, Lord of the Underworld wishes to take you, Persephone, as his bride, to rule alongside him faithfully and steadfastly as the Queen of the Underworld," Zeus announced pompously.

"Brother. My word. Hardly a romantic marriage proposal, eh?" Hades muttered, glaring at Zeus with an enormous sigh. "By heavens, I know you are King of the Olympian Gods, but couldn't you at least let a guy make his own marriage proposal?"

Sophie found her cheeks burning. She definitely felt light-headed now. She was afraid she would faint. She picked up her glass of water and took another gigantic sip.

"Be my guest," Zeus made a dramatic sweeping bow. "Do it now."

Sophie snuck a glimpse at Hades. He was looking at her intently, his eyes searing with what looked like rage, or … agony. She could not be sure. She was suddenly reminded of the picture she had taken of him, buried deep in the camera roll in her phone. There was something of that expression there as well – concern, or worry, perhaps. She willed herself to regulate her breathing and hoped fervently that she would not faint.

"This is hardly the way I wanted to ask you," Hades began, addressing her, his voice softening considerably. "I'm sorry, Sophie. I know this must be bewildering for you. This is hardly a romantic, or even remotely appropriate situation, but I have no choice. I would like to say to you now that … if you would have me, I wish for you to be my wife; stay with me by my side, help me run the often chaotic and infuriating realm of the dead, be with me every day and every night, and allow me to make you happy, safe and beloved, for as long as we exist."

Sophie's breath caught in her throat. She did not in her wildest dreams expect that Hades was capable of saying such tender words. She could feel her eyes filling with tears and she fought hard to keep them from falling down her cheeks. If she were an ordinary woman, facing an ordinary man, she would be immediately shrieking her affirmation and jumping up to embrace him jubilantly. He would laugh and catch her by the waist, swinging her round and round until they both collapsed in a heap from giddiness. She would kiss him full on his lips, secure in his love for her, and hers for him.

But she knew she was not an ordinary woman, and he was certainly no ordinary man. The catch was coming.

Zeus cleared his throat. "Yes, thank you, that's very nice. So, Persephone, the thing is, your mother Demeter belongs to the realm of the living. She will not be able to follow you into the Underworld should you choose to accept Hades' proposal. You will never see her again."

Demeter spoke. "I wish for Sophie to stay with me, until the day I breathe my last."

Sophie turned to her mother, completely shocked. Her mother had uttered a coherent sentence, in the context of a current conversation! It had been such a very long time since she last even remembered her mother doing so. Sophie gazed longingly at Demeter, tracing with her eyes the lines of her perfect heart-shaped face and the white hair pulled neatly back into a bun at the nape of her neck. Sophie had sworn to herself that she would take care of her mother and stay right by her side for as long as she lived. Hearing her speak brought on a wave of nostalgia so strong it blindsided her. For such a very long time, it had been the two of them against the world. And then, when she was diagnosed with the disease, Sophie *was* her entire world. She knew that her mother needed her. They were bound together by the red thread of fate for a lifetime. That was the way Sophie saw it, and she could imagine no possible universe in which she abandoned her mother. As with Hades, she, too, had duties to fulfil.

Zeus cleared his throat again.

"I see that we have reached an intractable disagreement between both parties. In my name as Zeus, God of the Sky and Thunder, and King of the Olympian Gods, I decree that Persephone shall alternately spend sixty years here on earth with her mother Demeter, and sixty years with Hades as

Queen of the Underworld, *ad infinitum*, or as long as your stories are being told, whichever is sooner."

He turned to Demeter. "You will have your daughter with you for the remaining of your lifetime in this mortal form."

He then looked to Hades searchingly. "Are you willing to wait for the sixty years that Persephone will spend with her mother? Is your love strong enough to withstand that?"

"I will wait. After sixty years, I will come back to the mortal realm to claim my bride."

"Hades, my good brother, you have to vow to stay guard over the Underworld for as long as Persephone is with her mother in the realm of the living. I will not accept another travesty such as the recent pandemic ever happening again. It is completely unacceptable and an utter disgrace. Hades, I know you well enough to trust that you understand exactly what I mean," Zeus said, boring his gaze into that of his brother.

"I understand," Hades replied. "If this horrific disaster had been in any way caused by what I did or did not do, I am deeply regretful. No mortal being should have had to die before his or her time, simply on the whim of a minor goddess."

He looked right at Demeter when he said it. Demeter stared fixedly back at him, not moving a muscle. Sophie looked from one to the other, not understanding.

"Hey, the lady hasn't given an answer to your proposal, you know?" Hermes suddenly piped up, his eyes alight with mischief.

Sophie looked down into her lap. A million thoughts raced through her head. It seemed so definite, so inevitable. She appeared to have no other choice at all. As hard as she racked her brains, she could not think of a better alternative. Then again, how could she possibly out-think wise old Zeus himself? She sighed and gave up thinking.

She turned her gaze to Hades. Her heart felt it would burst at the sadness and trepidation she saw in his face. He looked utterly dejected.

"Hades, my answer to you is *yes*. I want to be your wife," Sophie said softly, wishing she could hold him and comfort him until that glaze of sorrow disappeared from his eyes. She then turned to Zeus. "I accept your ruling, Sir. I will spend sixty years with my mother among the living, and sixty years with my husband among the dead, perpetually, time after time, for as long as I am Persephone, she Demeter and he Hades."

Zeus looked satisfied with her answer. "That's my good girl," he said fondly, ignoring the pointed sidelong glare shot his way by Demeter. "Right! That's settled, then!"

He looked down at his aggressively expensive watch. "And still in good time for me to attend Dionysus' yacht party! Excellent."

Sophie felt very tired all of a sudden. All she wanted was a hot shower and a good long sleep. She knew that the heartbreak would come, but at that moment, she could not feel anything. She looked around the room dazedly, sensing a deadening stupor coming over her. It was as though she was looking at the world from an oddly detached, disembodied standpoint. A view from nowhere.

Zeus' expression softened ruefully as he watched her little face grow paler and paler. "Don't you worry. Hermes will escort you and your mother home. Everything's going to be fine. Be strong, my dear girl."

"Sir, may I … may I at least say goodbye to Hades?" Sophie asked politely.

"Yes, yes, of course! Hermes, take them into the garden," Zeus boomed.

Hermes was gentle as he took her elbow and slowly guided her to her feet. Sophie shook her head, as if to physically empty it out. She was acting like an invalid. She had to pull herself together. She needed to be strong, for her mother.

"I'm fine, thank you," she smiled at Hermes, who nodded graciously and pointed the way with an outstretched hand.

Hades and Sophie followed as he led them through a fairly labyrinthine corridor ending in a quaint little garden. It was small, but shrouded with great big trees for privacy. There was a set of baroque garden table and two chairs, as well as a white Victorian-styled swing set.

"I'll leave you two to it," Hermes winked and disappeared back into the house.

Hades and Sophie faced each other. Words seemed insufficient to convey how they felt at the moment. They lapsed into a small silence.

"Oh look," Sophie said softly. "It's that rare type of house sparrow, with their little white chest feathers."

Hades looked. She was right. In contrast to the predominantly brown Eurasian tree sparrows commonly found in Singapore, the house sparrow had a lot more white on its body, with its partial brown bits draping along the back of its head down to its tail like a cape. The sparrow cocked its head inquisitively at them, and flew away to land on the graceful arch of the swing set.

Seized by a temporary urge of madness, Hades picked Sophie up in his arms and carried her over to the swing set. He set her down gently on one side and took the seat on the opposite side. They sat there for a long time, face to face, letting the swing rock them gently in the windless night. It was dark outside, but the powerful street lamps from the street gently illuminated the garden. It was an unobtrusive, diffused glow that lent the simple backyard an atmosphere of warm cosiness. Sophie looked up at the faint dusting of stars that smiled down at them. She was sure most of them were actually satellites.

Finally, she spoke again.

"Will you still remember me, after sixty years?"

"If I forget, will you help me to remember? Will you make me fall in love with you again?" Hades said teasingly. However, Sophie looked so distraught that he hastily added: "I'm just joking! Sophie, now that I've met you, how could I ever forget you?"

Sophie fell silent. She knew what he meant. It was one thing living her life, *before*, not knowing he existed. But now that their paths had crossed, how could life ever be the same again? Her heart was screaming in pain, but the tears did not come. Not yet.

"Thank you for that lovely proposal, by the way," Sophie said lightly. "I will never forget a single word you said."

"Uh oh. *I've* already forgotten what I said," Hades put a hand over his mouth.

They both tried to smile.

"You know what? Goodbyes really suck," Hades announced.

"Yes, indeed," Sophie agreed. "This isn't goodbye. I'll be seeing you again. If you don't forget me, that is."

"Perhaps you would be the one to forget me."

"I'll issue you a challenge then. Eat six seeds from a pomegranate every day for sixty years, and see if you'll forget me," Sophie raised her chin defiantly.

"I will, if you do it too."

"Yes, I accept the challenge."

"Then I accept it too."

They grinned at each other.

11 FORGIVENESS

The bedroom door creaked slightly as Hanna closed it behind her as quietly as she could. Sophie's mother had fallen asleep after eating her lunch. There was a light breeze blowing. The soft strains of the radio trailed away as she brought the bowls and utensils back to the kitchen. She loved this time of the day, when her patient took a nap and she had a spot of free time to scroll around her phone aimlessly.

Unbeknownst to Hanna, the patient in the bedroom was going on a sojourn, albeit not in her human form. Demeter left her human shell behind, ensuring that it still made the requisite movements of mortal sleep. The soft rising and falling of the chest; the occasional toss and turn; the intermittent snore. She was good at what she did. Slipping into a cat's jaunty silhouette, Demeter squeezed through the window that had been left slightly ajar. With the slightest flick of her tail, she was gone.

The cat meandered the human streets unheedingly, stopping once in a while in quiet corners to groom itself. It relished the stretch in its powerful muscles, the precision and nimbleness of its small neat paws, and the freedom to roam the neighbourhood undisturbed. She jumped from high place to high place. She sprinted up stairs three at a time.

She nonchalantly walked the narrow ledge of a ditch, barely using any conscious effort to maintain balance. The cat was one of Demeter's favourite forms to take.

Before long, despite having taken her time to savour the journey, she had reached her daughter's flower shop. Hopping up onto the window sill, she settled into her usual spot to watch the goings-on in Sophie's World. To any passer-by who noticed her, she was merely a stray cat starting her usual grooming ritual. The cat licked her paws and assiduously scrubbed her face, the back of her head and then her ears. She twisted around to lick her shoulder blades and her back, taking the time to ensure every strand of fur was evenly combed. If she felt like it, she moved on to her forelegs and then to both flanks and hind legs, and ended with her tail from tip to end. Typically, when she had moved on to the filing and shaping of her claws, the bamboo wind chime would sound, signalling the arrival of a customer.

Sophie found herself looking at the photograph of Hades on her phone again. It had been almost six months since they parted, but she still could not bring herself to remove the second apron that hung beside hers on the wall. It waited patiently on its hook, as if anticipating the familiar swipe of its owner's large calloused hand. Sophie imagined she could feel the pathos of the garment, as it woefully awaited the call to serve its master once more. It even looked sad from the way it drooped from its hook, lifelessly gathering dust.

Sophie rubbed her eyebrows with the back of her hand. She was projecting her own emotions on inanimate objects again. She smiled a little at her own sorry state. On a whim, she took down the apron that once belonged to Hades and put it on instead of her own. She tried to remember the way he smelled, the lines of his body. The timbre of his voice was starting to fade away from memory. It was becoming less and less real, like something she had once heard in a dream. The photograph in her phone seemed like the only evidence she had that proved his existence. Sophie put her arms around her own waist and hugged her body, wrapped in the apron that was too big for her. She raised its neckline to her nose wonderingly, but it smelled of nothing more than dried flowers and emptiness. There was a familiar pain that rose within her body, starting from the depths of her abdomen, shooting upward violently and flowering amply in her chest. Sophie doubled over, clutching herself helplessly as she slid into a crouch on the ground. The tears had dammed up a long time ago, but the pain came back every so often, catching her off-guard at the most unexpected moments.

Her breath had caught in her throat and she was finding it harder and harder to breathe. She wished she could cry; it would at least release the tension in her oesophagus, in her clenched gut. Sophie could feel some heat building up behind her eyes, but it was as though the mechanism for producing tears was broken. No matter how much her chest hurt, the tears would not come to take the pressure away.

"Breathe properly," she rebuked herself fiercely, hugging her knees to her chest. Her heels were lifted high above the floor to help her keep her balance. She felt safe, being close to the ground. If she were to fall, it would not be from such a great height.

Sophie closed her eyes, stuffing her nose into the gap between her knees, and tried to concentrate on evening out her breathing until the waves of pain went away. They always did, eventually.

"It's just pain," she whispered urgently to herself. "It's just pain."

Don't think about him. Just don't. Sophie thought she might break into pieces if she allowed herself to wallow in memory and self-pity. *It's just pain. A physical, bodily pain. It hurts right now. It hurts so bad. But it will go away soon. It's just pain.*

The bamboo wind chime sounded. Sophie stood up abruptly, letting go of the fistfuls of apron she had not realised she had been clutching. Stars danced across her vision from standing up too quickly. She held on to her work table for dear life.

"You have to help me! I need this urgently!" the customer who had just entered the shop implored. Her voice was coarse and unbridled. It was the kind of voice that was used to getting exactly what it wanted.

Sophie looked up. A nondescript woman dressed in a white top and black pants barrelled her way up to the counter. She was short and unremarkable-looking, so her commanding voice seemed slightly at odds with her countenance. She reminded Sophie of a matryoshka doll. Perhaps there were ever smaller versions of her nested infinitely within, all of them contributing their voices to the booming amplitude of the whole.

"What is it, Madam? How can I help?" Sophie asked.

Without invitation, the matryoshka doll flung herself onto a seat at the counter.

"A funeral wreath," she said matter-of-factly without preamble. "I need one as soon as it's humanly possible. By this evening. If not, tomorrow morning."

"Hmm, that I can do," Sophie answered pleasantly. "My schedule is clear for today, fortunately."

"Thank you so much!" the matryoshka doll seized Sophie's hands in hers, theatrically. "You're a lifesaver."

"By the way, I'm so sorry for your loss. May I know who it is that you are ordering this wreath for?"

"It's my mother."

"Oh dear!" cried Sophie. "I'm so sorry to hear that. I can't imagine what you must be feeling."

For the first time since she strode purposefully into the shop, the matryoshka doll looked introspective. She expelled a huge sigh.

"It's complicated. We're estranged," she continued most impassively. "I suppose you might find it strange for a daughter to be sending a wreath to her own mother's funeral wake. The thing is, I've not even seen her in thirty years. I wasn't there when she breathed her last. I had even contemplated not attending the wake at all. But some things have happened since, and I guess I've had ... an epiphany of sorts."

"Oh dear ..." Sophie paused, trying to process the information. "I don't know what to say ..."

"The wreath. Please make it for me, as a symbol of my ... forgiveness. That is what I need."

"Of course, I can do that. Forgiveness … Do you mean to say that in life, your mother had wronged you?" Sophie boldly ventured the question that was on her mind.

"That she had, certainly!" the matryoshka doll laughed drily. "Gosh, I would kill for a smoke right now."

Sophie caught that small twitch of the fingers toward a trouser pocket. In a lightning-fast second, Sophie weighed the pros and cons in her mind, and heaved an internal sigh of resignation.

"Well, one here is okay with me. A secret between you and me," Sophie said cheerily, with a wink. She ducked under the counter and strode over to crack open the window nearest to them. As subtly as she could, she also crept to the door and flipped the little plastic sign around, indicating that the shop was CLOSED.

"Just one, I promise," the matryoshka doll winked back, her fingers immediately extracting the cigarette pack from her pocket.

Sophie mentally groaned but was careful to keep up a serene visage as she rooted around for an empty drink can to serve as an improvised ash tray.

"Oh, by the way, how may I address you? My name is Sophie," she said, determined to get the image of the matryoshka doll out of her head.

"I'm Hilda," came the answer, chasing after a languorous spiral of cigarette smoke. "Thanks for this, I really appreciate it."

She gestured carelessly with the cigarette. Sophie fought with all her might not to wince as she watched the flecks of ash scatter happily over her precious pinewood counter.

"Will you tell me your story?" Sophie asked brightly. "It would help me with conceptualising an appropriate floral arrangement for your specific needs."

Hilda took a long drag on the cigarette and blew the smoke towards the ceiling.

"Of course. It's no spectacular story. I've had a difficult relationship with my mother ever since I was a child. She was a housewife, her sole duty was to take care of me and the household. But as far back as I can remember, she was drunk more than half the time. She would beat me for all sorts of trivial matters and verbally abuse me. It got so bad that she started leaving visible bruises on my limbs that my teachers at school noticed. I remember two of them coming to visit us at our home. I hid in a corner as they talked to my mother. I remember feeling so ashamed ... that I had troubled my teachers to come all this way just to talk to my mum, all because I was a naughty girl. I genuinely believed, back then, that I deserved all the punishments she meted out."

Another long drag on the cigarette and Hilda continued. "My father was away a lot. He had to work overseas, in Indonesia, for months at a time. Whenever he returned, my mother would be on her best behaviour, and I would enjoy pockets of heaven as she temporarily stopped beating me or hurling curses at me. But then Dad would have to go away and she would start all over again. It became almost amazing, how creative her methods of torture would get."

Sophie could not help but cover her mouth with shock. "That's really terrible to hear."

"For what it's worth, my mother kept me alive despite it all. She fed me, clothed me, sent me to school. There was nothing I lacked. On hindsight, some sanity, perhaps," Hilda paused again, quirking her lips into a sardonic smile. "It was not until I turned fifteen or sixteen that I finally broke. She was in a particularly bad mood – over *what* I cannot for the life of me even remember now – but she hit me so hard that I went flying into a bookshelf and broke my nose. There was blood everywhere. My eye started to puff up like a balloon. I was told later at the doctor's, that I had a hairline fracture on my jaw too. It was the proverbial last straw. I left the house and never went back."

Sophie pressed a fist to her forehead, at a loss for words.

Hilda smiled wanly, waving her dwindling cigarette about. "Don't worry about it. It was such a long time ago. My father tried to persuade me to come home and to reconcile with my mother. But I was young and stubborn. I refused at every count. For years I slept on countless couches of charitable friends … until I was old enough for boyfriends, and thereafter, I bounced from one man to another, all while working my butt off and furiously saving up for an apartment of my own. Fortunately, my father continued sending me money throughout my schooldays until I graduated. The moment I started working, I told him to stop. I told myself that I never wanted to have to depend on anyone for shelter ever again. I could not allow anyone that power over me, never again."

"And you achieved it," Sophie said.

"Yes, yes I did," a gleam of pride came into Hilda's eyes. "I moved into my own apartment when I turned thirty-five. I had boyfriends when I pleased. I was alone when I wanted. I kept in touch with my father via the occasional phone call, but never saw my mother again. Throughout all the phone conversations I had with my father over the decades, he never once mentioned her. And she never tried to get me back. I knew that I was right – she never wanted me at all."

Sophie swallowed hard. It was such a sad and lonely life story.

As if reading her mind, Hilda laughed heartily in what Sophie came to recognise as her signature bawdy, unguarded manner.

"Don't you go feeling sorry for me now, Sophie!" she said, dropping the cigarette butt into the aluminium drink can. "I love my lifestyle. I love my independence and my freedom. I'd not given my childhood a moment's thought until days ago, when my dad called me to tell me that my mother was in a bad way. That if I wanted to see her for the last time, it would be my only chance."

Sophie fiddled with the containers of floral teas lined up beneath the counter out of nervous habit. "And ... you chose not to?"

Hilda absently rattled the drink can containing the lone cigarette butt. "I chose not to. At the time, I did not see the point in it. For thirty years, we led separate lives. She was a stranger to me by then. And ... I suppose, despite the long passage of years, I had never truly withdrawn my resentment and ill will towards her."

She sighed. "But then, she passed away, and my dad called me again, asking for my help with the funeral arrangements. He sounded really lost and distraught on the phone. He could not manage it all on his own. That was when it suddenly dawned on me that he was an old man now. So, of course, I agreed to help. And for the first time in thirty years, I went back to the apartment where I grew up."

Sophie inhaled a sharp intake of breath.

"Yup," Hilda sighed again. "She still lived there even after I had left home. With my dad, most probably. I don't know what became of the state of their marriage, since he never mentioned her in his phone calls to me. And I had never asked."

"What was it like, returning to the place where you were abused?"

"I felt nothing as I made my way there. It had been such a long time ago. But the moment I stepped into the house, it was as if I were a child all over again. The feelings of fear and oppression and helplessness all came flooding back, as fresh as if it had all just happened yesterday. There were some small changes in the furniture and appliances, but everything looked almost exactly the same as it did when I lived there. The hatred, the fear, everything came back."

Hilda paused, setting the drink can down on the counter. "But then, my dad started talking to me. He told me about the last few decades of my mother's life. She had dedicated all her time to volunteering for their church. He told me that she prayed to the Lord every night to seek forgiveness for her sins. But she never once asked to contact me. To seek *my* forgiveness. Dad said she probably felt that she did not deserve my forgiveness. She had not even wanted to try. She was too ashamed, my father said. She believed that getting in contact with me would do more harm than good. I spent hours with my dad tidying her personal effects. There were countless photographs of her on mission trips to rural corners of the world. So many bibles, rosary beads. There were neatly copied recipes on scraps of paper for her food contributions to church events. She had nothing of luxury, nothing of excess. It was then and there that I decided that I *had* to forgive her. I wanted sincerely to abandon all the resentment and anger and negativity I felt towards her. There was no need for apology. There was no need for retributive justice, no need for punishment. I did not even regret the fact that we did not reconcile. There was a feeling of peace that came over me – I would simply forgive who she was and whatever had driven her to do what she did to me."

Sophie remained silent for a long time, thinking about Hilda's words. She, too, felt the peculiar and rather counterintuitive sense of completion and closure to her story. There had been no teary reconciliation. There had been no apology given and none accepted. But yet, she understood, as Hilda did, that things could not have gone any other way than they had. Given who she was, given who her mother was, this was the only possible ending to their story. Was it right? Was it justified? Was Hilda morally blameworthy in any way? Sophie did not think she was in a position to pass judgement.

And so she started making the wreath. That was all she, as a mere florist, could do.

Instead of the laser-focus that usually characterised her work, Sophie found her mind wandering a little this time. She could not help but think of her own mother. Since that day at Zeus' vacation home in Sentosa Cove, troubling thoughts nagged at her incessantly. The thought that her mother had not been truthful to her. The thought that her mother was possibly at the moment still not being completely honest with her. The thought that the person she was so close to had turned out to be almost a stranger. The confusing fact of her mother's real identity. The little inconsistencies that begged to be unravelled. Sophie had been sitting firmly on the lid of a giant can of worms. She was afraid to open it. She did not particularly *want* to open it. She did not want any truths to come to light that would dim her love and respect for her mother.

Must I open the can of worms? Must I investigate every single suspicion I have, must I throw a searchlight in every murky corner? If she did not do so, would it mean that she lacked self-respect? That she was morally infirm in some way, a weak fool with no desire to defend herself? *Must I be angry, to preserve a sense of self-dignity?*

Despite the roiling of her mind, her hands worked precisely and methodically, well-honed with years of muscle memory. They flew effortlessly around her tools, her flowers, her workspace, pulling into being the requested funeral wreath as though with a will of their own. Her hands created a huge Christian cross out of white chrysanthemums and cleverly hidden wiring, accentuated with soft pink roses and lilies. Silver coin eucalyptus leaves and monstera ferns added structure and gravity.

As the wreath of forgiveness took shape, so did Sophie's thoughts on her mother. *No, I am not morally obliged to be angry.* Like Hilda, she could choose to forgive her mother, be it for truths she withheld, or for transgressions she performed without Sophie's knowledge, or, quite simply, for the kind of person she was. There was no need for apology, or a demand for explanation, or letting the past congeal into some fixed and permanent wrong. Even before they arose, Sophie could choose to relinquish ownership over the feelings of resentment, desires for retributive justice, or even desires for deserved punishments. *Does this make me a coward? Perhaps. Does this mean I am in denial? Perhaps.*

I will be this happy coward, in denial, who will simply focus on fulfilling the responsibilities that are truly my own, Sophie thought. *I will simply act in reaction to my mother's choices, and let her lead our relationship wherever she deems fit and proper. This is my duty as a daughter, and nothing more.*

The wreath was done. The two women sat in silence for a moment, taking it in as it sat innocuously on the counter. Sophie felt an odd duality, as though she had made the wreath as much for her own living mother as it was for Hilda's departed mother. The forgiveness was both Hilda's and her own.

"The white cross is perfect. I suppose, in her twilight years, she had become quite the pious and faithful child of God," Hilda broke the silence. "Thank you, Sophie, for capturing my sentiments so precisely."

"Thank you, Hilda, for coming here today."

Epilogue

The old lady swayed gently in her rocking chair. A children's picture book lay open on her lap. The afternoon sunrays slanted in through the window, illuminating the dust motes and warming her toes on the wooden floorboards.

She felt sleepy. Her eyes slowly drifted shut.

But, at that moment, a great chasm split open in the ground, and out sprang a splendid black chariot, edged with gold, pulled by four strong horses. Hades jumped off the chariot, bident in hand. He was clad in an imposingly resplendent outfit that looked like dress uniform straight out of a Russian tsarist regime of old. The light danced over the shining gold of the fringed epaulettes, round buttons, ornamental braided cords and the sash that crossed his torso.

"Long time no see, Sophie," he said softly.

She opened her eyes.

The man from her youth stood before her, unchanged, ageless. At the moment, all thought flew out of her head as she simply looked at him. The memories came flooding back. The day they first met; the feel of the hard ground beneath her knee as she had crouched beside him to take his arm. The months he had spent working at her flower shop, his warm presence like a constant spring breeze beside her. That particular way he scrutinised her face, searching intently for the true emotions she sometimes hid from the world. Their first and only date; the shape of his hands in hers as they watched the sun melt into the sea. The look on his face that evening in Zeus' garden, where they had bade farewell.

"It's you," Sophie whispered, her throat dry. "I'd begun to wonder if I had merely imagined having met you at all."

The Lord of the Underworld reached out his hand. She took it.

As she stood up from the rocking chair, the years dropped away and she became a young woman once more. A white wedding gown swirled into existence, flying around exuberantly to fit perfectly on her trim little figure.

"I had Madame Coco Chanel herself design that for you," Hades added, trying to impress.

Sophie laughed. He was just as she remembered. The cadence of his voice, the way he made the room feel so small. Despite herself, tears started coming to her eyes.

"Are you really ... here?" she asked wonderingly. "I shall be most cross to wake up and find that this is only a dream."

Hades abandoned the casual, light-hearted demeanour he affected.

"Come here," he grabbed Sophie by the arm and pulled her into a firm embrace. He buried his face in her hair. "I'm here, for real. You didn't imagine it at all. The years have been long and difficult for me and I've missed you. I hope you didn't have to suffer too much. I hope you led a happy life."

Sophie clutched him tight. He smelled just as she remembered. It was both comforting and overwhelming at the same time. To her great embarrassment, her tears were quickly morphing into histrionic, full-bodied sobs. She covered her face with her fingers, all while desperately trying to sniff the free-flowing mucus back up her nose.

"I was … it was …" she started, but was unable to form a coherent sentence. Her chest began to ache from all the sobbing, but she did not know how to stop the tidal waves that rose deep from within her.

Hades held her head to his chest, not moving. The feel of her small body against his was almost too much for his heart to bear. He stroked her back briskly.

"Shh, I'm here now. I'm here for you. Don't cry, Sophie."

He waited patiently as her tears eventually subsided.

"We're … we're together again," Sophie said tentatively, looking up at him.

"Yes, yes we are! Come, Sophie, look, I dressed up specially to look handsome for you," Hades said, trying to lighten her mood. He held her at arm's length so she could see his outfit and executed a natty little spin.

She gazed wonderingly at the huge bident in his hand, forged from pure gold from tip to tip. It looked heavy. The double prongs were scorching red at its ends; she wondered if she imagined the heat and steam that seemed to emanate from them.

"You look … very nice," Sophie said, smiling a little shyly. "All you need to complete the look is that navy blue apron. Maybe … I like that old look a little better."

"I know you do," Hades said softly.

The look in her eyes made his heart ache anew. Hastily, he looked around the room. It had remained almost exactly the same as he last saw it, except for heaps of books crowding the table. Many of them were about classical Greek mythology.

"I have to look the part, don't I, as King of the Underworld here to claim my bride," Hades said. "You're looking at me like a cat that's got a mouse. Are you sure you're still the same sweet Sophie that I remember?"

"I suppose you'd just have to find out for yourself," Sophie said as calmly as she could, while sniffing violently again with both her hands covering her nose.

"Yes, you're right. You're stuck with me for the next sixty years," Hades said ominously. "I will follow you everywhere you go until you get most sick of me."

"Better you than pomegranates," Sophie said darkly. "I regret having made that challenge."

Hades laughed heartily. "Come on then, Queen of the Underworld, we've got a wedding to attend!"

"Whose wedding?"

"Ours, of course!" Hades said witheringly. "Shall we go now, please?"

"Oh, wait!" Sophie clasped her hands to her chest. "Will you give me a moment to make a fruit basket for Cerberus, please? I want him to try all the yummiest tropical fruits."

Hades sighed theatrically. "Alright, alright. Hurry up, will you? This outfit was not made for Singapore's damned humidity."

"It won't take long," Sophie said as she scurried off to the kitchen, the long train of her white wedding gown trailing behind her like an ethereal gathering of sunny day clouds.

Hades laid a hand on the neck of one of his horses. They were whinnying and stamping their feet impatiently. It was a very tight fit for them in that bedroom.

"We'll be home soon, boy," he clicked his tongue gently, brushing the horse's mane with generous strokes.

The horse scuffled at the fringe of the epaulette on his shoulder, huffing out warm air. Its eyes were alert and intelligent. All four of them were magnificent horses, the best of the best in Hades' stables. They made little stomping sounds on the ground and tossed their manes this way and that, eager to serve their master.

"I suppose you lot have to get used to the dilly-dallying of your new mistress, boys," Hades said softly to the horses. "She's always puttering about, busying herself with little things to make someone or other happy."

"Are you already complaining about your wife so soon?" Sophie said as she came back into the room, holding a basket full to bursting with rambutans, longans, bananas, jackfruit, guava and a few others that Hades could not identify.

"You're going to get Cerberus fat!" Hades exclaimed. "Don't spoil him. He's a working dog after all."

"Don't worry! He's got three heads! That's three times the food a normal dog would need," Sophie said, her eyes gleaming with happy anticipation. She adored dogs.

"You're more excited to see him than to see me," Hades complained.

"You know that's not true," Sophie smiled. She set the basket down on the empty bed and took Hades' hands in hers. She stood up on tiptoes and hesitantly touched her lips to his. "Let's go home, Lord of the Underworld."

Hades helped her into the chariot, mindful of the copious reams of lace and fabric.

In the blink of an eye, the room stood empty, holding nothing but the wind. Beyond the lowered shutters of the window, a black cat with strange eyes sat at the common corridor, grooming itself diffidently.

The afternoon was unusually hot for that time of the year.

~*~

Sophie hooted with delight when they arrived.

Hades hoisted her down from the chariot. They stood in front of a door with a signboard emblazoned 'SOPHIE'S WORLD'.

"Oh," Sophie hesitated. "I've stopped running the shop for, I don't know, at least twenty years now."

"I know," he said. "This is an exact replica of what I remember of the shop, made for you right here in the Underworld. This will be your very own sanctuary, where you can always come for a respite, for when you need to catch your breath."

"From the tiring business of running the Underworld, you mean?"

"That, amongst other things, too," Hades' eyes gleamed playfully.

"Hmm," Sophie smiled.

"Let's go in," Hades said, reaching down to take her hand. He opened the door for her and motioned for her to enter.

Careful not to step on the long train of her dress, Sophie walked slowly into the flower shop. She was startled as a burst of applause and riotous cheering greeted her.

"Sophie! Welcome home, Sophie!"

She allowed her eyes to adjust to the relative dimness of the interior. She gasped as she saw the shop packed wall to wall with familiar faces, who were all so dear to her throughout her lifetime. There was Mr Chang, grinning ear to ear, holding on to Amanda's waist. There was Anne and her little boy Benton, still clutching a toy fire truck. There was Hanna and a man who had to be her husband, his arm slung carelessly around her shoulders. There were countless other customers who had become extremely close friends throughout the long journey of her life. They had all departed first, one after the other, gradually leaving her more and more alone.

But now, here they all were, beaming broadly and shouting her name. The flower shop looked exactly as it did when Hades was working for her. He had remembered every little detail of its interior décor – the little special handmade touches she treasured so much, the bamboo wind chime, the sounds, the smells, everything. She saw two work aprons hanging neatly side by side on the wall by the cashier's till, as they did six decades ago. The counter, the tall stools, the little windows that offered just the slightest glimpse of the world outside …

Sophie could not bear it. She dissolved into tears once more and crumpled into an ungainly squatting position, hiding her face in her hands.

"Sophie! Don't cry, Sophie! We're all reunited now!"

"Sophie, we've missed you!"

Hades had entered the shop, closing the door firmly behind him. He crouched down in front of Sophie and tenderly pulled her hands away from her face. Using his fingers, he wiped the tears away from her cheeks.

"You know, I wasn't hoping to make you cry when I made this," he whispered to her.

"No, I'm sorry, I'm just so happy. It's perfect," Sophie struggled to compose herself. "Thank you so much."

He pulled her lightly back on her feet. "Come! It's our wedding day! Let's celebrate!"

The cheering intensified, almost deafening in the small enclosed space. Someone brought out the champagne, causing a huge commotion.

Hades pulled Sophie to him, clasping his hands over her head protectively. "I love you, Sophie. Thank you for being my bride."

Sophie raised her face to him. "I love you too, I always have and always will. This will never change; no, it can *never change*, in fact, because someone has dreamed us into being."

Hades smiled. He thrust a hand into his pocket and retrieved something.

"What's that?" Sophie peered curiously.

He opened his hand, and there, sparkling in his palm, was nestled a pair of rings. They were a brilliant gold; their bands painstakingly carved with mysterious, intricate patterns.

"No offence, but I didn't trust old Chang's taste in jewellery. I had Hephaestus himself make these for us," Hades beamed.

"Hephaestus ... God of Metalworking?"

"I see you've been doing some homework. Yes, he's the god of blacksmiths, metalworking, carpenters, craftsmen, artisans, sculptors and metallurgy."

"Oh," Sophie inhaled. "I would love to meet him."

"I'll see what I can do. He's one busy guy," Hades said.

"Of course."

"Alright, alright, stop fawning over another god," Hades said, in mock sternness. "This is *our* day."

"Yes," Sophie smiled. "You jealous?"

"Of course! You are my wife."

"Mm … say that again," Sophie closed her eyes happily.

"Persephone, my wife, my queen," Hades said obligingly. He wrapped both hands around her delicate little neck and kissed her deeply. They hardly heard the ruckus and roar of approval that exploded around them.

As they separated, Hades took Sophie's left hand and slipped the smaller of the two rings steadily onto her fourth finger. She took the other ring from him. Her hands trembled like autumn leaves in the wind as she slid the ring onto his finger. Her vision was swimming in a colourful blurry haze.

Hades tugged at her hands. "Sophie, don't close your eyes. Look, I've made a present for you."

He had unearthed a bouquet from a secret hiding place in the shop. It was an extremely valiant effort, with lavish blooms of all kinds, each competing loudly for attention. It looked as though he had tried to cram the most number of different flower species possible into one huge bouquet, all tied vehemently together with a thick ribbon, sitting slightly askew. The piece looked extremely precarious, as though it were held together by sheer force of will and a very hopeful reliance on the strength of the ribbon.

Sophie could not help but convulse in laughter.

"Sorry, I realised that I didn't know what your favourite flower was. So I just incorporated as many types as I could," Hades said, rather guiltily.

"Florists don't have favourite flowers," Sophie reassured him, taking the bouquet from him very carefully. She thrust her nose into the riot of blooms and took a deep breath. It smelled of happiness. "Thank you, Hades. This is a really good try."

"Perhaps I should just stick to being a deliveryman," Hades chuckled.

"I could teach you the secrets of my trade. *If* you have time for mere hobbies, that is," Sophie added.

"I'll always have time for you. *Always*," Hades said, locking eyes with her steadily.

"Be careful of what you promise, in front of all these witnesses," she warned. "They're all on *my* side."

The crowd bellowed with laughter appreciatively. Hades swept a lock of hair from her face tenderly.

"Alright, teach me the art of flower arrangement. Teach me all about the different types of floral teas. Teach me how to listen to people like you do, to sense their needs and to fulfil them. Teach me the light of the living."

Sophie smiled happily. She hugged the bouquet close to her heart.

"I will. I have a good pupil," she said. "And please teach me how to rule fairly and justly. Teach me how to judge appeals. Teach me the names of all the rivers in the Underworld. Teach me how to walk amongst the different geographical regions and to know who belongs and who does not. I want to be a good queen for you."

"Yes, I will do all of that," Hades responded. "But first! To the marital chamber!!!"

The congregation erupted into a frenzy of wolf whistles.

ABOUT THE AUTHOR

Yihan Sim was born in 1991. She is the author of *Fear of the Guest*. She graduated from the National University of Singapore in 2015 with a Bachelor of Arts with Honours in Philosophy. Her interests include classical Greek philosophy and Zen Buddhist philosophy. She lives and works in Singapore.

Persephone's Choice is her second novel.